Petteril's Wife
Lord Petteril Mysteries
Mary Lancaster

Petteril's Wife

Chapter One

"Cor," said Piers Withan, Viscount Petteril.

It was hardly his usual expression of awe, but the sight of Lisbon from the River Tagus seemed to merit something special. A beautiful, white-washed city rose grandly up from the water's edge, spilling over several hills into the distance. Elegant domes and spires reached up into a sky of unchanging blue. The sheer loveliness took his breath away.

Beside him at the ship rail, his assistant April nudged his elbow. "I believe you need to adjust your language, Mr. Whittey. Unless we are swapping places."

"You are quite correct, Mrs. Whittey," he replied, dragging his gaze from the city to her no less beautiful face. Her golden fair hair was elegantly pinned behind her head. A wide-brimmed straw hat with blue feathers and ribbons tipped forward over her face to shade her complexion from the hot sun and sea breezes. Her deep blue eyes, however, danced with mischief, making his lips twitch. "Although it might be fun."

"Swapping places?" she asked with a hopeful glint. "Can we?"

"Not this time," he said with some regret. "We have a serious task ahead of us."

April turned back to face Lisbon. "Yes, but have you ever seen anywhere more beautiful?"

"I don't believe I have."

"You'll change your mind quickly enough when we get ashore," said their fellow passenger, Lieutenant Roberts, grinning with a hint of pity at their naivety. He, returning from England after medical treatment, had passed through Lisbon twice before.

"Never, sir," April said fervently.

She carried off this masquerade as a lady perfectly. No one would have guessed from her confident posture that she had never worn such fine clothes before this voyage, or from her speech that she had grown up on the back streets of London docks and St. Giles. She had always been an excellent mimic and by now, since Piers made her keep the accent even when they were alone, she hardly ever slipped. The occasional word of thieves' cant had popped out once or twice, but in refined tones and fortunately not in the presence of anyone who understood.

Piers was both amused and delighted. He did not allow himself to analyse that delight too closely, contenting himself with acknowledging its usefulness in their quest.

Lisbon only grew more beautiful the nearer they sailed.

"If I was Major Withan," April whispered, "I'd lose myself here too and never leave."

Piers didn't put it past his hedonistic cousin Bertie, except that desertion from the army was both serious and dishonourable and Bertie rather needed the adulation of his peers. Piers wished he was here merely for pleasure, but perhaps there would be time later...

The harbour, where ships of war were tied up beside merchantmen and fishing vessels, was bustling with activity and colour. Cargoes were loaded and unloaded amidst multi-lingual shouting. Soldiers in reds and blues and greens flowed off ships into the organized chaos of the quay.

But it was not just the light and bright clothing that fascinated Piers. Under the blazing sun, with April's hand in his arm, pinching and wriggling against his sleeve in excitement, he walked off the ship and up the steps onto dry land and into an enchantingly foreign country.

For once, he found the sea of faces greeting him more interesting than overwhelming. Besides, he had no need to recognize any of them.

Instead, he could simply enjoy the sheer melting pot of races and cultures swarming around him.

"Senhor Whittey, Senhora, welcome to Portugal," said the official, barely glancing at their passports. He was too used to British documents passing through his hands and a mere Mr. Whittey, a clerk, and his wife, were not important enough to stir any interest. Lord Petteril would no doubt have been a different matter—which was how he had acquired these alternative papers from an old friend in the Foreign Office, who perfectly understood the danger to Bertie and the need for secrecy.

Lieutenant Roberts, with whom they had made friends on board the ship during their ten day crossing from England, commandeered a rickety conveyance which he called to them to share.

"I'll drop you at your hotel," he offered, "on my way to report. Latour's is pleasant enough and I'm sure the Envoy's staff will direct you to decent accommodation of a more permanent variety."

Even the air smelled different—humid and exotic. And, as they left the sea breezes of the docks behind, the scents became less pleasant.

Piers's nostrils flared. "A bit whiffy, isn't it?"

Roberts grinned. "Told you. And this is where the upper orders live. Best avoid the poorer areas—makes you gag. Stinks of garlic and rotting food, and the streets are like sewers—begging your pardon, ma'am."

April, who was perfectly used to fetid back streets, didn't look particularly interested. She was all but hanging out of the window to look at everything they passed and exclaiming in wonder. She looked so vital and charming that it was no wonder the lieutenant watched her, smiling a little. He was just a little in love with her, which made Piers uneasy.

It was not far to the hotel, where their modest luggage was quickly unloaded. April smiled prettily at Roberts and gave him her hand to bow over. Piers shook hands, thanking him for his help and wishing him good fortune.

As the conveyance drove off, an African young man in light trousers and a belted tunic helped them carry their luggage inside.

"You want to see the city, I take you," he offered in English with a huge smile as Piers dropped a coin into his waiting hand. He then vanished, presumably before the hotel staff chased him.

A clerk was hardly paid enough to splash out on separate sleeping accommodation for his wife, so Piers had insisted merely on a decent room with a dressing closet. After nine nights spent in the same cabin as April, he was sure they would both relish the privacy. In fact, their dressing closet turned out to have a truckle bed made up, presumably, for a servant, which would be bliss after a bench with his legs dangling off the end. April had fought him over the bench, of course, shocked that the viscount should endure such hardship while she had all the comfort.

She fought him over the dressing room too.

"It ain't right," she said mutinously. "And it's your turn for the comfy bed."

"Ain't?" he repeated, dropping his trunk onto the truckle bed to settle matters.

"Is not," she muttered, glowering.

"Get changed, then," he ordered. "We can have tea before I call at the Envoy's residence."

She brightened at once, all but gurgling with delight. She was like a little girl revelling in the joy of dressing up and playing at tea parties. It made his heart ache for the childhood she had never had.

Even now, she never lost herself completely. "I'll see what I can find out here while you're gone," she murmured.

This was the hotel Bertie had stayed at when he landed in Lisbon, and he had apparently abandoned some of his things here, although they had been removed by the Envoy so that the room could be re-let.

"Good plan. Don't go out without me."

She, perfectly used to looking after herself, cast him a glance of tolerant scorn.

Receiving directions from the hotel staff, Piers crossed elegant streets and squares to the Envoy's residence, seeking the shade of trees whenever he could, for the sun was relentless. Even so, he was sweating profusely by the time he arrived.

The Envoy's office was unexpectedly busy. Men who would have fallen over themselves to serve Lord Petteril in any way they could, were quite happy to make Mr. Whittey, newly posted clerk, kick his heels indefinitely.

Eventually, a flustered but efficient man in his thirties called him to a desk and shook hands briefly. "Whittey, yes, we've been expecting you. I'm Jonathan Jeffery, secretary to His Excellency."

Mr. Jeffery flapped his hand at the seat on the other side of the desk and accepted Piers's letter of introduction with a quick frown. The frown only deepened as he read.

"Your primary task," he said, raising his eyes to Piers's face at last, "is to discover what you can about Major Albert Withan's disappearance?"

"That is correct."

"It's not what we were told in the first place. And, forgive me, what do our lords and masters in London imagine you can discover that we who have been here for years cannot?"

"Who knows?" Piers said apologetically. He was used to polite contempt and had learned to use it. "My only advantage is that I can devote all my time to the matter, which is a luxury I doubt anyone else has."

"I am happy to co-operate in any way I can," Jeffery said, folding the letter and handing it back. "But in all fairness, I have to tell you that Major Withan is very probably dead and his body unlikely to be recovered. Lisbon is not like home, Whittey. Bad things happen all the time, especially in the back streets where it is criminally foolish to venture after dark. Or before, come to that."

Piers forbore to mention that bad things happened in London's warren of back streets too. "I do understand that, but his family is insisting on further investigation."

Jeffery curled his lip. "A viscount in the family makes all the difference."

"I'm afraid it does," said the viscount sympathetically. "The news of his disappearance apparently hit the dowager viscountess, Major Withan's aunt, very hard, and his lordship was most insistent we pursue the matter further. Could you tell me all you know about what happened?"

"Certainly, though it is very little. Withan landed on the first of June, reported to all the necessary authorities and stayed at Latour's hotel while he waited for orders to join his brigade. He was given such orders and was due to leave for Cuidad Rodrigo on the morning of 7th June. But he never reached Cuidad Rodrigo or caught up with his brigade. It transpires that Captain Hood, who was to have been his chief traveling companion, assumed Withan was with some lightskirt and would catch up en route. So Hood left without him, taking the other soldiers and horses with him. It was more than a day after arriving at Cuidad Rodrigo before he reported Withan missing. Thought he was covering for his fellow-officer who was probably already dead."

"So Withan never left Lisbon?"

"We don't know with certainty whether he did or not. No one seems certain whether or not other horses were requisitioned. He had clearly taken most of his kit from his room, but not all—though what he left was packed into a small bag. The hotel manager tells us no one saw him leave and he never paid his shot, which is not uncommon among the entitled though Lord Wellington doesn't approve. Nor does the Envoy, since we have to work with the Portuguese on all levels."

"I believe you have what he left behind. May I see it?"

"You can have it," Jeffery said. "Send it to his aunt Lady Petteril. Or the viscount himself."

"Thank you," said the viscount meekly. "According to my masters at the Foreign Office, there is some fear of a ransom demand."

Jeffery shrugged. "It is possible, if someone kidnapped him, knowing who his family is. There are groups of bandits who keep reforming between Lisbon and military theatres in Spain. So, especially if he set out alone on the journey, he *could* have been taken. But we've received no ransom demand and we're already well into July, so I would doubt it. On the other hand, they may have sent directly to Lord Petteril. Perhaps you should have checked before embarking."

"I did and there was nothing, though that was ten days ago now." Piers tugged thoughtfully at his lower lip. "I don't suppose you know which lightskirt Captain Hood meant?"

Jeffery was amused in a sardonic kind of way. "My dear Whittey, bordellos are ten a penny in this city. I doubt Hood ever knew. Frankly, I doubt Withan did! Is there anything else I can tell you?" Jeffery began gathering up his papers. "I have an appointment with His Excellency."

"Of course," Piers said. "I would just ask if he has friends in the city I might call on? Either Portuguese or English?"

Jeffery scowled impatiently. "How should I know? I saw him at the opera once with the Condessa de Cartaxo. Oh." Half out of his seat, Jeffery sat down again. "Between ourselves Whittey, I've been trying not to think about this, but the morning of the 7th, when Withan should have left Lisbon, the Conde de Cartaxo's body was discovered in the street outside a brothel. He had been stabbed to death. The Portuguese never found his killer and are never likely to—these things happen every night though not generally to the nobility."

Piers's eyes widened. "You mean Withan fled after murdering this conde?"

"It has been suggested," Jeffery muttered. "Don't believe it myself. Whatever else, Withan was a gentleman. If he was responsible, it would have been a duel, though why either should chose to fight in such a location is beyond me."

"They could have been drunk as wheelbarrows," Piers allowed.

"Only explanation if it's true. Personally, I'm not convinced it is. I'm pretty sure he's dead, whether here in Lisbon or out of it. Look, Whittey, if you're really going to pry into this, you should try to understand the underlying politics of the people concerned. I'll send a man to you this evening with Withan's effects, and he'll explain further."

Jeffery rose and there was nothing for Piers to do but rise with him and return to the hotel.

HE FOUND APRIL JUST outside Latour's front door in conversation with another African youth—or it might have been the same one for he was certainly dressed similarly. Piers had a problem with faces. April obligingly solved this one for him.

"Mr. Whittey," she said, greeting him with her usual sunny smile. "This is Dado—Eduardo—who so kindly helped with our bags earlier."

Smiling, Dado tugged the brim of his hat. "I show you the city? Cathedral and castle? Opera?"

"Perhaps later. We're expecting someone."

"Dado was telling me about the English officer who vanished into thin air," April said with manufactured horror.

"Pff!" said Dado throwing open his hands. "One night here, then gone. No one ever see him again."

"Major Withan?" Piers said. "I heard about it at the Envoy's office. A warning to us all. Did you know the major, then?"

"Yes, I show him Lisbon, I take him places he not know."

"When was the last time you saw him?"

"The evening before he vanish."

"On the 6th of June?"

"*Sim.* Yes."

"What was he doing?" April asked, her expression one of avid awe, waiting to be thrilled and shocked.

"I don't know. He go off to meet someone."

"With his trunk?" Piers asked.

Dado grinned. "No. He meet a lady, I think—he buys flowers from the seller on the corner and put one here." He touched an imaginary lapel.

"What time was this?" Piers asked.

"Evening," Dado replied vaguely.

"Did you see him come back?" Piers asked.

"No. I go home before that. I don't expect to see him again because he go to Spain next day. Then an English officer ask me about him, and I learn no one see him since I do."

"Which officer?" Piers asked.

Dado thought, taking off his hat to scratch his head and putting it back on again. "Captain... Captain Everett."

"I don't suppose he is still in Lisbon?"

"I still see him on his crutches sometimes. Good fellow. He waves to me. I take you to see him?"

"Why not?" Piers said. "Can we walk?"

"Sure."

Chapter Two

April was thoroughly enjoying herself. Even under such scorching sun, she loved wearing her soft new clothes, a plain gold ring on her finger and in the evenings, a necklace of beautiful pearls or the gold one with sapphires. In her previous life she had never dreamed of wearing such luxurious items, having only ever glimpsed them passing through the hands of thieves and fences.

Even more than the clothes, and the gentlemen bowing to her, she loved walking on Lord Petteril's arm, eating meals with him, talking to him about everything. She had loved the intimacy of sharing a cabin with him on the ship, even though he had insisted she sleep on the bed as a real wife would, while he stretched out half-on, half-off the uncomfortable bench at the foot—although a real husband would not.

She had enjoyed falling asleep to the sound of his breathing, rising to the knowledge of his presence, and the sound of his voice. Though she tried not to, she sometimes pretended to herself that she really was his wife, a bittersweet pleasure, even if only for a few moments.

Always honest with herself, she didn't much care if Major Withan was alive or dead. She didn't like him. He had done his lordship many bad turns, and if she had been the major's cousin, she would have left him to rot. His lordship, however, was of a more generous nature, and April was certainly intrigued by the mystery. And glad that if Major Withan had never done anything else useful, he had at least given April the opportunity to go abroad with Petteril.

She had been thrilled and flattered that he wanted her with him. And though she knew it was largely to help with his affliction about faces, it was also because she had helped him with previous mysteries. And because, somewhere both beneath and above the rules of the world, they were friends.

For propriety's sake, she could not travel alone with a single gentleman, and so the comical masquerade of the married couple began. They shared the secret joke, addressing each other as Mr. and Mrs. Whittey—the name being chosen for its closeness to Petteril's family name of Withan.

He had largely shed his viscount's hauteur, returning to his more natural academic character while she played the ambitious lady of some middling rank—which she had been practicing with some hilarity anyway, ever since she became unexpectedly reunited with her old friend Annie the courtesan. Petteril had trained her more ruthlessly, pulling her up for every slip and making her keep in character for hours at a time before they left England, and every day, all day, since. Sometimes, she even caught herself *thinking* in the nobs' accent, and giggled.

And now she was trying to keep up with other people's foreign accents, and even a new language where she and Petteril began, for once, as equals.

As they walked arm in arm in Dado's wake, he told her in low tones the little he had learned at the Envoy's office, including the death of the Conde de Cartaxo, which might just be associated with Bertie's disappearance.

"Do you think he did it?" April asked.

"Not without a dashed good reason," Lord Petteril said. "Bertie has a very strong sense of survival." He wrinkled his nose as a gentle breeze, which would otherwise have been most welcome, wafted a foul stench of food and human waste in their direction.

The streets were much quieter now. In fact, they seemed to be the only people around, their footsteps echoing eerily along the roads. Presumably everyone was avoiding the heat which, if anything, was more intense than when they arrived.

Captain Everett was discovered in a house that appeared to have been taken over as a home for convalescent officers. He seemed delighted to see them.

"Anyone found Withan?" he asked Dado hopefully. He was a pleasant looking young man of medium height, with brown curly hair and a snub nose.

"No," Dado said, indicating Petteril and April, "but they also look for him."

As Dado turned to leave again, clearly knowing his place, April, who had never known hers, itched to take out her notebook and pencil from her reticule and take notes. Remembering her new role, however, she curtseyed to Captain Everett's bow.

"Whittey," Lord Petteril said, shaking hands. "And my wife."

"Everett, captain in the 52nd." Seizing the walking stick propped against his chair, he limped to the door and yelled into the depths of the house in Portuguese before turning back to his guests. "It's hot for walking," he observed. "Especially if you've just landed. Please, sit down, ma'am."

Unwilling to take the captain's chair when his leg was not healed, April whisked over to the window seat. A servant appeared with a tray of lemonade and wine in jugs and three glasses and departed again.

"So what's your interest in Major Withan?" Everett asked, pouring the refreshment, which April seized with a relief that approached joy.

"I've been sent to find him," Lord Petteril said. "He has friends in high places."

Everett nodded sagely. "Cousin's a lord. How can I help?"

"According to Dado, you are a friend of his."

"Amusing fellow. Eager to get to action. Been a Hyde Park soldier all his life and bored to tears."

April exchanged glances with Lord Petteril. If Bertie was still looking forward to military action, he would hardly have deserted.

"When did you last see Major Withan?" Petteril asked.

"The evening before he was due to leave. Sixth of June? Came and hauled me off to drink wine with some other friends, about five or six of the clock, then brought me back here. I was still using crutches then—dashed tiring way to get about, so I appreciated the company."

"Was he always so helpful?" Petteril asked, not troubling to keep the surprise from his voice. Bertie Withan was almost entirely self-centred.

Everett grinned. "Not always, but I suspect he was on the way to a lady."

"What lady would that be?"

"Couldn't say." Everett took a long drink but found, when he lowered the glass at last, that Lord Petteril's steady dark gaze was still upon him. "Well, I can't!"

"Being a gentleman," Petteril said, "who does not bandy a lady's name about. I too am a gentleman of discretion, and my wife never gossips except to me. In this case, for Major Withan's sake, I believe you have to tell me the truth."

Everett sighed. "I don't actually know the truth. To be frank, I didn't really know Withan—he was only in Lisbon a few days and I've been on the peninsula for nearly two years. He thought I knew the ropes, as it were, and my confounded leg was taking forever to heal. I was bored and glad to show him what I could of the town."

"Carousing," Petteril translated.

Everett grinned.

"Where did you carouse?"

"Several places. He took me to a condessa's ball once, and to the opera another night, but apart from those, you might call the rest houses of—er…decreasing respectability."

"Which condessa?" April asked.

"The Condessa de Cartaxo. Beautiful lady—almost as beautiful as you, Mrs. Whittey."

April laughed. "Was it the condessa he went to see the night before he left?"

Everett opened his mouth, closed it again, then, running his fingers through his hair, said, "It might have been. There was another lady he admired too, Senhora de Almeida—although her daughter might have been the true attraction."

"Busy man," Lord Petteril commented, "considering he was only in Lisbon a few days."

Everett gave a lopsided grin. "You don't know the half of it. They were his more respectable pursuits."

"There were other girls," Petteril guessed, "in the back streets? Perhaps even in the one where the Conde de Cartaxo met his end?"

Everett flushed, glancing uneasily at April. "If you know so much, why are you asking me?"

"Because I don't know. I'm only guessing."

"I don't believe for a moment that Withan had anything to do with the conde's death."

"Did you take Withan to that—er...house?"

"Once," muttered Everett. "To be more accurate, Dado took both of us."

"Could you take me?" Lord Petteril asked.

Everett's jaw dropped.

To April's amusement, a tinge of colour crept along his lordship's cheekbones.

"To speak to the girl concerned," Petteril said hastily. "It's possible she was the cause of any quarrel, whether it involved Withan or not."

"Oh. Of course. I'm sure the Portuguese authorities will already have questioned them."

"They might not have asked the right questions," April remarked, setting down her empty glass beside her.

"These people don't like questions at all," Everett warned. "The conde is far from the only man who's died in these back streets since

I've been in Lisbon. It's more than possible poor Withan is another. You really don't want to go there, Whittey."

"You could just give me the address," Petteril said mildly.

"Actually, I couldn't. If it has one, I don't know it." He sighed. "I could take you there, but Dado had better come with us and, if possible, some fighting fit officer, fully armed!"

"I can't just now," Petteril said, standing up. "We have an appointment soon. But if you will permit, I'll call on you tomorrow."

"Thank you for the refreshment," April added. "It was just what I needed."

"IF BERTIE DID KILL this conde, for whatever reason, would he really have run away?" April asked.

Back in their hotel room, April had collapsed on the sofa, her hat and reticule beside her. Lord Petteril, coat abandoned, was lounging against the rail of the shaded balcony, only just within her view. He appeared to consider.

"If he kept his boyhood characteristics," his lordship said at last, "he is more likely to have brazened it out or lied through his teeth. On the other hand, he is in a foreign country, doesn't speak the language, and might not have trusted the British to back him against a powerful native family. Even if he did run, where would he go?"

"To one of his women?" April suggested, sitting up and dragging her notebook out of her reticule.

Petteril came back into the room, closing the French windows. "You mean someone could be hiding him?" he said thoughtfully. "Not for ransom but for love?"

"It's a possibility," she insisted, writing the latest information and her own thoughts in the notebook. Both the speed and the formation of her letters was improving all the time.

Before she had met Lord Petteril, only four months ago, she had never even written her own name.

"It is," Petteril agreed, sitting down beside her so that he could read what she was writing. "Only it would hardly further his ambition to fight the French. He'd be cashiered for desertion if he was ever caught. So the alternative must be truly dreadful."

She liked sitting beside him as though they were equals, though it was a touch distracting.

He stirred. "We don't know enough. We don't know any of the people involved with him since he came here."

"Except Captain Everett," April pointed out. "And we only have his word that Bertie left him at his lodgings and went on to meet some woman."

"You didn't believe him?" Petteril asked.

"Actually, I did."

Petteril sighed. "So did I. And his irritating reluctance to mention the ladies in question tends to speak in his favour rather than against him. Shall we go out to dine?"

Dining with his lordship, whether in private or public, was still such a novelty that she flushed with pleasure. "Do I need to change again?"

A knock on the door interrupted them. Lord Petteril rose and went to open it. A fussy, middle-aged man of some importance bustled in, shoving a bag into his lordship's arms. "Whittey? Kelvin, the Envoy's man. Major Withan's effects."

"How do you do?" Petteril murmured. "Allow me to introduce Mrs. Whittey, my wife."

Kelvin, the Envoy's man, spared April a glance and then a longer one. April didn't like him, both because of that longer look and because of his dismissive rudeness to his lordship whom she clearly deemed beneath him.

"Some refreshment, Mr. Kelvin?" April asked, rising to bob the smallest curtsey.

"Sadly, I have no time, ma'am. Perhaps you would give us the privacy necessary for me to educate your husband? Before he crashes into affairs of which he is necessarily in ignorance and causes a diplomatic incident I have to spend the next three months dealing with."

"Then I withdraw the offer," April said coldly, walking past him to the bed where Lord Petteril upended the bag full of Bertie Withan's "effects". He did not look in the least offended by Kelvin's manner, more interested in raking through the little pile on the bed.

April ran her hand around the inside of the bag, but there seemed to be nothing else.

"A comb, a book, a letter from Lady Petteril," his lordship murmured. "Otherwise, this looks like his laundry—two shirts, a nightgown, some undergarments, two neckties and a couple of handkerchiefs. Is this all you found?"

"It's all he left," Kelvin said impatiently. "He must have taken his trunk with him."

"Then you subscribe to the theory that he left Lisbon?"

"And was waylaid by bandits on his way to Cuidad Rodrigo, yes. I'm afraid he brought it on himself by not traveling in company with Captain Hood and the other soldiers. In short, Major Withan was an arrogant sort."

"The hotel staff did not see him leave," Petteril pointed out.

"The staff are always busy," Kelvin snapped. "And since he did not pay his shot, I daresay he was anxious to leave unseen."

"Uncharitable," his lordship murmured, turning to face Kelvin once more. "Don't you like him?"

"I never met him."

"I see," Petteril said.

Kelvin's eyebrows flew up. "And what exactly do you see?" he asked testily.

Petteril did not answer directly. Instead he said, "You all speak of him in the past tense. You, Mr. Jeffery, Captain Everett. You assume he is dead with no evidence and no reason."

"No evidence?" Kelvin looked about him exaggeratedly. "If he is not dead, where is he?"

"If he *is* dead, where is he?" April countered.

"Good point," Lord Petteril murmured, while Kelvin glared at her as though she had grown horns.

"Our private talk, Whittey," he commanded.

"Oh, you may speak before Mrs. Whittey."

"Such matters bore the ladies," Kelvin said.

"*The ladies* need not concern you. Mrs. Whittey is aware that the major is something of a rake. Do sit down."

Kelvin condescended to sit on the sofa. Petteril handed April into the chair opposite and leaned his hip casually against the arm.

"We diplomats," Kelvin began portentously, "walk something of a tightrope here in Portugal. Britain needs this base to continue fighting Bonaparte. And not all the Portuguese are grateful for our help in pushing the French out of their country. Some did better under the French, such as the Conde de Cartaxo. You see why some might imagine the British are happier with him out of the way."

"Are we?" Lord Petteril inquired.

"No. To be frank his death is a nuisance we could do without. Our people already kept an eye on Cartaxo and concluded he had changed his sympathies with the regime. Certainly he has put supplies Wellington's way, and ours too."

"So Major Withan had no motive for killing him?"

"No, but since he was pursuing Cartaxo's wife, the conde might well have the motive for a fight."

"I gather the major also pursued other women."

"Senhora de Almeida. Besides some back street doxies. Senhor de Almeida," he continued, "is also an important man in the Portuguese government. He is very pro-British, and we do not wish to ruffle his feathers."

"Would he be prepared to ruffle ours over Major Withan's behaviour?"

"Senhora de Almeida is a virtuous lady. A great lady, even. She knows how to behave, and so does her husband."

"Did Cartaxo?"

Kelvin met his lordship's gaze superciliously. "Of course."

"Would you introduce me to the condessa? And to the Almeidas?"

Kelvin rose to his feet. "I will not. I am far too busy to conduct your social life. Besides, I cannot imagine either family would accept introduction to so minor a functionary."

"They must deal with clerks and secretaries all the time," the viscount said modestly. "I engage not to invite any of them to dance. If you are too busy, Mr. Kelvin, perhaps you could spare a moment to write down the addresses of both the condessa and the Almeidas?"

April rose and indicated the desk between the two windows, where a sheet of paper and a pen-stand with ink awaited. With ill grace, Kelvin wrote two addresses in perfect script.

"Thank you," Petteril said.

Kelvin glared at him. "And you are not to harass the poor, widowed condessa."

"Does she blame Major Within for her husband's death?" Petteril asked.

"I never heard that she did. Don't let us down, Whittey." And with a nod to April, he walked out without shaking hands.

"What an unpleasant, self-important little man," April remarked, then recalling a few past encounters with London's underworld, she added, "Perhaps you should be a more *dangerous* clerk the next time you meet him. What shall we do now?"

"Dine," said Petteril.

Chapter Three

Piers woke the following morning from an excellent sleep in an actual bed. Even the heat had not kept him awake, and he was hopeful of the various clues he had learned yesterday.

Accordingly, he sprang out of bed without having to listen first to discover exactly where April was or in what stage of ablutions or dressing. Yet as he splashed cold water over his head and body, in perfect solitude, it struck him that he might actually miss that odd dance of propriety in their ship's cabin—squeezing one's eyes shut or hastening in or out of clothes in the gloom and going up on deck in the rain to let her dress in private. There had been an odd companionship in it, and pleasure that she trusted him. And all without discussing it.

His original plan had been to go first to this brothel Bertie had frequented and call on his more aristocratic acquaintances later. However, a glance at his fob watch showed him he had slept rather later than he meant to. Perhaps they should catch the condessa between breakfast and *sesta*.

When he rapped on the dressing room door, April called cheerfully for him to enter the main bedchamber. Dressed in a charming shade of jonquil, smiling and hatless, her eyes gleaming with delight in her surroundings, she was momentarily more dazzling than the morning sun.

"This is such a beautiful place," she enthused, keeping to her nob's accent. "I wish London was like this. Where are we going first? To the condessa's?"

"Breakfast," Piers replied, as his stomach rumbled. "En route to the condessa's." She was hardly dressed for a condolence call, but she looked so pretty that he said only. "Bring the black gloves."

They broke their fast at a little baker shop with a table beneath a shady tree. Used to a more substantial breakfast, Piers was at first disappointed to be presented only with new bread along with thin slices of cheese and cold meat and olives. However, the bread was warm and delicious, and he found when they had eaten the lot that he really didn't want any more.

The sun was getting ever warmer as they walked on, away from the stenches of the city to the sea and along the coast to the wealthier district of Belem where the Condessa de Cartaxo resided.

Her house, built like much of Lisbon in a rather lovely classical style, was set back from a tree-shaded street, surrounded by a pleasant garden with orange and lemon trees and a riot of bright pink flowers. Had Bertie walked up this same path, swaggering with confidence? It seemed so likely, Piers almost felt him there. Involuntarily, he glanced up at the shutters, most of them flung open to air the rooms before the fierce heat of the sun grew too intense. Only one attic room had its shutters still closed. But then, mere servants probably lived up there.

The door was opened at once by a dark-haired, sallow manservant.

"*Bom dia*," Piers said civilly, presenting one of the plain cards he had had printed in London.

The manservant appeared to sneer at the card, then summoned a maid who took it from him and scampered off. The manservant remained at the door, gazing somewhere above Piers's head.

"Beautiful garden," April commented.

"Isn't it?" Piers agreed.

He was relying on the condessa's curiosity to be allowed to speak to her, but it was perfectly possible she had none and would refuse them. With no obvious signal from within, he was almost surprised when the manservant opened the door wider for them to enter and led the way along a wide but gloomy passage to a room at the back of the house.

The apartment into which they were ushered was a glorious surprise. Well-proportioned and sunny without being hot—floor-length lace curtains covered the windows— it was full of colour and beauty, from the hangings to the bright vases, flowers and ornaments scattered about the furniture.

The condessa herself, dressed all in black silk and lace, rose from her chair.

Oh yes, Bertie has been here, Piers thought cynically, for the condessa's loveliness hit one hard and instantly. Thick, raven black hair, piled high on her head with a jet comb, perfectly arched black brows and long lashes framing melting dark eyes, a complexion that might have been considered sallow in England but was somehow perfect here, and an expressive, somehow sensual mouth.

"Mr. Whittey?" she said in a smooth, husky voice like hot chocolate. "I am the Condessa de Cartaxo."

"My wife, Mrs. Whittey," Piers said. "Please accept our condolences on your recent loss. I hope we do not intrude too painfully?"

"If you did, I would not receive you. Tea, José." She smiled faintly. "You see, I know what our English guests like. Please, sit and tell me how I may serve you."

"I'm very glad you speak English so well," Piers said, aiming for a diffident but charming smile, "for I would struggle horribly otherwise."

"My husband and I have many English friends, including the British Envoy, Sir Charles."

Was that a warning that there would be consequences to encroaching? "It is about an Englishman that we wished your advice and insight."

"That is most odd of you when the city swarms with fellow English."

"Indeed. But we believe Major Withan called upon you, the night before he disappeared."

Sitting down, she smoothed her skirts, hiding her eyes, deliberately or otherwise. The tea was brought in then with commendable rapidity. While the condessa spoke of the weather and the crowds in the city, a maidservant poured the tea and passed the cups before departing.

"Major Withan," the condessa repeated at last. "We knew him, certainly. And yes, he did call on my husband and me to make his farewells."

We knew him. She too spoke of him in the past tense. Did she know he was dead? Piers's last male relation by blood...

"His family made such a fuss that I have been sent from London to investigate," Piers said apologetically. "And to find him, if possible."

The condessa's gaze lifted to his, her eyes dark, mysterious, intense. On some level, she cared. "You believe he is still alive?"

"I hope so, though I am slightly alarmed by how many people assume he is not."

"There are bandits in Portugal and in Spain—guerilla fighters, deserters, outlaws of every persuasion and none. If he never reached Cuidad Rodrigo, it is a reasonable guess—but no, not a certainty—that the poor man is dead."

"That is what I have heard," Piers admitted. "But his family would like proof."

"He is of noble family?" the condessa asked.

"His cousin is a viscount," April said in an awed voice that drew an amused and faintly contemptuous glance from the condessa.

"Is that so, senhora? Do you always accompany your husband about his duties?"

"Oh no, condessa! But I could not let slip the opportunity to come abroad with him. Lisbon is so beautiful."

"In parts," the condessa said languidly.

"May I ask how you met Major Withan?" Piers asked.

"At the opera. Sir Charles Stuart introduced us."

"And when did you last see the major?"

"As you said, the day before he left. He came to say goodbye early in the evening."

"Was he in good spirits?" Piers asked.

She smiled. "Very much so. I never saw anyone so eager to be shot at. And I believe he planned to be carousing for much of the evening."

"Did your husband go carousing with him?" Piers asked.

She held his gaze. "No, not that I know of, though they may have met up later. Our own authorities asked me the same question. I don't believe for a moment that Major Withan murdered my husband. Why would he? They were gentlemen, friends, and allies."

"Of course," Piers murmured. "Do the authorities have no idea who killed the conde?"

Her gaze dropped. "None."

"Who do you think did it?" Piers asked.

Her eyes flew back to his, widening in surprise. "I? What would I know of such matters?"

"Condessa. In my experience, wives know everything, however little they say. My own wife is a perfect example."

"I am," April said. "And men should stop thinking of us as fools."

The condessa blinked. "Sadly, it is our only advantage, senhora."

"Not the only one," April said judiciously. "Do you have any idea where Major Withan went after he left you?"

"You might ask his friend Captain Everett."

"We did," Piers said.

The condessa sighed. "Sadly, I can add no more." She rose to her feet in clear dismissal. "I hope you will call again. Widowhood is lonely, and I would like to know how your investigation progresses."

"Thank you, condessa," Piers said, bowing. "Oh, one last question, if you would be so good. When the major called on you that last evening, was he wearing a flower?"

The condessa blinked. Piers touched his lapel to show what he meant, and she frowned as though genuinely thinking about it.

"No, I don't believe he was," she said at last.

WHEN THEY HAD GONE, Condessa Beatriz de Cartaxo gazed rather thoughtfully after them.

Even for English people, they were an odd couple and she found it difficult to label them. He spoke like a gentleman and she like a lady, and they were clearly comfortable together. There had been no ex-changed glances, no unnecessary touching as they sat side by side on the sofa, and yet there had been understanding between them. She stayed quiet while he asked his silly questions—that were not, after all, quite so silly—until she chose to push a point, and he let her.

It was a kind of wordless understanding she had once hoped for with Severino and never achieved. Well, she never would, now. Though she was still young enough to marry again...

From her sleeve, she took out an elegant lawn handkerchief, em-broidered with the initials A.J.W – Albert John Withan. For a mo-ment, she let her mouth droop with genuine sadness. She had even seen a certain likeness to Bertie Withan in the features of Mr. Whittey, the mere clerk from the British Foreign Office presented with an impossi-ble task.

He was already defeated, although he didn't yet know it. Poor Whittey.

Poor Bertie.

She shoved the handkerchief back up her sleeve and walked out of the room. She climbed the stairs slowly, in anticipation of *something*. Good or bad, she wasn't sure which.

"NOT SURE WE LEARNED very much," April complained as they retraced their steps.

"She is hiding something," Piers said.

"You don't expect her to admit to being Bertie's lover, do you?"

"No, but..." His frown deepened. "Did she look grief-stricken to you?"

April thought about it. "Uncomfortable," she said at last, "beneath her languid manners. But not inconsolable for her late husband. They probably don't make love matches here. And whether or not they were lovers, she didn't have much time to fall in love with the major, did she?"

"No. He had enough time to offend her though."

April's jaw dropped. "You think he did, and she croaked him for it?"

"*Croaked*," Piers remarked, "is not a ladylike expression, even when uttered in the accents of a nob."

"Nob isn't a gentlemanly word either," she retorted.

"Neither it is. No, I don't think she murdered him for being offensive. But her husband might have."

"A duel?" April said, staring. "Outside a brothel?"

"We need to inquire."

"Can—*may*—we stop for another drink first? I want to write down exactly what she said before I forget."

"Yes." He drew her hand into the crook of his arm. "We may."

WHEN THEY RETURNED to the hotel, April said, "Dado is back." Glad to have her confirmation of the African man's identity, Piers ambled up to him where he lounged in idle conversation with several other men.

Dado smiled spontaneously, as though pleased to see him, and tugged his hat to April.

"Will you go and fetch Captain Everett?" Piers asked, dropping a coin into his palm. "And bring him here if he can manage it. Whether or not, he comes with you, I'd like to hire your services for the afternoon."

Dado looked even more delighted and took off at a run.

"I'm not staying here," April informed him as soon as they were inside their room, "while you go to the brothel. I know these places and you don't."

Petteril, who was flicking through several items of post delivered to him when they entered the hotel said, "I'm not planning on going inside if I can avoid it. I want to see where Cartaxo died, and hopefully find someone who—er...knew Bertie. I'm sure if we lurk in the street long enough, they will come to us."

"Maybe. I'm still not waiting here."

"Then you'd better change into something less gorgeous."

To his secret delight, she blushed with pleasure, laughing to cover the fact. "I've still got Ape's clothes."

"No, you haven't. I removed them from the trunk. The calico print and a dark shawl will do." Throwing aside two of the letters, he broke the seal on the third. A card fell out, which April picked up.

"What is this?" she asked.

"We are invited to the home of Senhor and Senhora de Almeida this evening."

"The major's other important Portuguese friends," April said, with excitement. "Why would they invite us?"

Piers laid down the letter. "Presumably because Kelvin—or more likely, Jeffery—asked them to. Interesting."

"Then we'll go?"

He heard the anxiety behind her eagerness. In a formal setting, she was afraid of letting him down. "Of course," he said casually, to show he had no qualms. "But first, a less salubrious excursion."

As he retreated to the dressing room, she called after him. "Better take your sword stick."

"I intend to."

Five minutes later—washed yet again and dressed in a lightweight, loose fitting fawn coat, carrying a tricorne hat of the same colour in one hand and his sword stick in the other—he emerged into the main bed-chamber.

April was admiring herself dubiously in front of the glass. In the less fashionable calico with just the light shawl over her hair, she looked endearingly waif-like, more like the April who, dressed up in women's clothes for the first time, had danced around his dusty attic.

"I look dowdy," she said, scowling at herself.

Amused, Piers said, "You don't. But considering where we're going, the dowdier the better. You keep close to me, and no wandering off."

"Don't worry, Mr. Whittey," she said kindly. "I'll look after you."

If Dado and Captain Everett were surprised by these changes in the Whitteys' appearance, they did not show it. Piers imagined that both Dado and the captain could pass unnoticed from the best areas of the city to the worst. British uniforms were everywhere, and so were the poor.

In consideration of Everett's still healing leg, Dado had hired a suit-able conveyance, which he drove. The carriage had open sides and a roof to protect the passengers from the sun. Everyone piled in and they set off through the city streets.

Away from the hotel and the more rarified opulence of Belem, Piers enjoyed once more the sheer life and colour of the city. His nostrils did flare involuntarily at the stench, and he was saddened by the number of beggars—many of them mendicant friars—but they too were part of the unique character of the place. It was clearly a very religious town, for there were innumerable churches of staggering beauty, as well as cas-socked monks, nuns and priests milling among the populace.

Traveling through ever-narrowing streets, he saw now that a great many of the whitewashed buildings that had so dazzled him from the ship, were in fact filthy and unrepaired. Their inhabitants threw their waste out of the windows into the street—including bodily waste by the stink of it. His stomach threatened to rebel.

Eventually, Dado stopped the carriage in the shade of an awning, and summoned a pair of urchins, to whom he tossed a couple of Piers's coins. Proudly, they took hold of the reins while Dado jumped down and opened the door for his passengers.

"We walk now. Sorry Captain."

"I'll cope," Everett said cheerfully.

With Dado and the captain walking ahead, Piers drew April's hand into the crook of his arm and they followed up the winding street, turned left up some steps, and then on through disgusting alleys that made Piers want to retch. The heat made the smell worse, of course. Even April, lamentably used to filth and squalor, wrinkled her nose, and grasped her skirts with her free hand to hold them out of the unthinkable, steaming filth lining the ground.

They emerged at last into a very slightly wider street where at least some of the rubbish had been swept away from a few front doors. Discreet businesses, Piers guessed.

Dado paused to talk to two women hanging out of windows on either side of the street to gossip. Piers paused to examine the nearest building. A thin, dangerous-looking man lounged on the front step, smoking a pipe. All the shutters and windows were open— some of the glass cracked, broken or entirely missing—except for one, fully shuttered, in the eaves.

A huddle of ill-dressed girls, their contrast to the modest dress of their respectable sisters only too obvious, dispersed, one swaying seductively toward Captain Everett. The others marched with clear hostility on April.

April, however, had lived close to prostitutes for much of her life and understood perfectly. Removing her hand from Pier's arm, she held it up in a gesture of peace, then showed them her "wedding" ring.

One of the girls laughed and said something that had her companions in stitches, too. Piers assumed they were speculating that April had brought her husband to them to be educated. Fortunately, Dado and Everett arrived beside them, presenting fresh meat to the women.

Dado spoke to them and a string of incomprehensible Portuguese rattled between them. All the women but one wandered off again.

Dado said, "The old women at the windows tell me this is where the Conde de Cartaxo is found." He pointed to the road under the brothel's windows, a few feet to the left of the front steps.

Piers moved, following his finger. "Here?" Compared with the rest of the street, the cobbles of this part had been swept fairly recently, but he still balked at the notion of lying down to demonstrate.

The remaining prostitute, a dark, slovenly beauty of indeterminate age, nodded vigorously. "*Conde. Sim.*"

"You saw him?" Piers said at once.

"Everyone saw him," said the thin man in the doorway in heavily accented English. He prowled the few steps toward them, outlining the shape of the body with the stem of his pipe as he went. "You buy the girls for more information."

"For more information, we keep the Portuguese and the British authorities away," Piers said pleasantly.

The thin man's eyes flashed malevolence. April was walking slowly around the shape he had described, peering closely at the cobbles. She scuffed at certain unrecognizable objects which had stuck there, kicking them to the side. Piers, catching on, fumbled for the quizzing glass hidden inside his coat, and, hitching his coat up, crouched down to examine the road more closely.

The Portuguese exchanged glances with each other. Everett frowned, uncomprehending.

At last, Piers raised his gaze to April's. "He was stabbed in the neck, and there is no blood."

"Perhaps they scrubbed it," April said without much conviction.

Only the rain had ever washed these streets and that was very unlikely in the summer. Plus, blood lingered notoriously.

Piers straightened and turned to Dado. "Will you ask them if they saw Major Withan the night before the conde's body was found?"

While Dado asked, fingering Everett's uniform coat by way of illustration, Piers watched their faces. The thin man, whom Dado called Lope, never looked anything but mean. Whatever Dado said, it did not appear to affect him. On the other hand, Piers could quite easily imagine Lope murdering his own grandmother for her handkerchief. The way he pushed aside the girl—presumably one of his own—betrayed a thoughtless cruelty. He could have killed the conde. He could have killed Bertie, especially if Bertie had run out of money...

The girl on the other hand, did react. She looked wearily sad as she spoke to Dado.

"Her name is Divina. She know Major Withan," Dado reported. "He come here that night, leave about ten."

Another two hours accounted for, Piers thought. Perhaps they were getting somewhere. "Was he well? Happy?" Piers asked her.

The girl smiled.

"Yes," Dado said.

"Did he pay?" Piers asked bluntly.

The girl laughed and nodded. Her left ear was torn, as though someone had cruelly ripped an earring from her lobe.

Lope spoke sharply to her and pushed her again toward the door.

"Wait," Piers said, raising his stick to separate them. Lope, not expecting the move, stared at him with more astonishment than anger. "Was the conde here at the same time?"

The girl shrugged.

Lope spoke angrily.

Dado translated. "He say conde never here, not that night or any other."

"Do you believe him?" Piers asked.

Dado's gaze flickered to Lope. He shrugged. "Yes."

Piers glanced around to ask April, then spun around on his heel. "Where is April?" he demanded, icy panic surging through his veins.

Chapter Four

Like Lord Petteril, April had noted the closed shutters at the top of the house. Whorehouses were not above imprisoning reluctant or recalcitrant prostitutes, and in such places no one cared about shouting or screaming, crashes or blows. It still made her angry. But at least now she was not powerless or afraid.

As Petteril asked his questions and Lope moved nearer to him, April took the opportunity of the now unguarded front door and slipped inside.

At once, she was overwhelmed by the distinctive, familiar smell, intensified by the heat, and had to fight the urge to bolt. Instead, she forced herself to run up the narrow stairs. She had to brush against a rather well-dressed gentleman coming down, but they didn't look at each other. Outside a door on the landing, a half-dressed whore leaned against one of the doors, smoking a cigarillo. She regarded April without interest.

April climbed the second flight of stairs, her skin prickling with memory and fear as she went deeper into the lion's den.

He's only on the other side of that wall, she told herself. *Many feet down, but still...*

Coming upon no one else, she eventually reached the top of the house and one closed door—presumably to the room with the closed shutters. Her heart drummed. She didn't know what she would find. An abused, imprisoned girl? Several? Or could it be Major Withan himself?

Lord Petteril did not really believe Major Withan was dead. Or didn't want to. His feelings towards his cousin were definitely mixed. Beneath the dislike and bad memories, she knew he did not want to lose this last male cousin, and that had nothing to do with the fact that Bertie was his heir. It was to do with blood and family and a shared, if distant, boyhood.

April turned the handle of the door, wondering what to do if she found either women or Withan. The door was locked.

She crouched down and with shaking hands felt for the calico bag hidden beneath her shawl. It contained a few small, dubious tools from her thieving past which had proved surprisingly useful in her new life as Lord Petteril's assistant.

The lock was not difficult. When it clicked open, she dropped the tools back into the bag and seized on a penknife she had brought from England, brandishing it in front of her like a sword as she straightened, and took a deep breath.

Surely they would never have kept Bertie here for so long? Either they would have killed him as a nobody or found a way to ransom him before this... *There'll be girls*. Like she had seen so often in reality and in her nightmares since. Like she might so easily have been...

She threw open the door and leapt back to avoid the brunt of any attack.

There was no one there. Only a few broken chairs, a narrow bed which had collapsed at one corner, with a mattress chewed to bits by mice. Or rats. No one aired the room because even here no one used it.

Slowly, she lowered the knife.

She was glad there were no abused women. On the other hand, it would have been lovely to have found Bertie Withan. Lord Petteril would have been so pleased with her he'd have forgiven her for wandering off.

Dropping the knife back into her bag, she left the musty, smelly room and closed the door softly behind her. Then she started back to the stairs, longing to be out of this place.

A man facing her on the gloomy stairs, halted, hurling sharp questions at her which she could not understand let alone answer. So she aimed for brashness. She had always been good at that.

"I go now," she said confidently, marching on.

He raised his hand to her with the clear, vicious intent of knocking her into the wall. But April had been dodging blows for most of her life.

Seizing the rickety banister, she vaulted, leaping through the air with flying skirts for the stairs below him. She landed lightly, if not quite like a cat, stumbling down a few more steps until she realized that in response to the first man's yell, another was running up toward the landing.

Trapped between them, April bolted into the nearest room, slamming the door behind her. Ignoring the couple on the bed who seemed as oblivious to her, she shot across to the open window and threw her leg over the sill.

God's bottom! There was nothing to hang onto to climb down, just a jump to the ground that would break her legs. Below, she glimpsed Dado vanishing around the first corner, Lope yelling into the house as Petteril advanced on him. She could not see his lordship's face, only his tension, until, before she could even yell, his head snapped up and he strode under the window, dropping the stick.

"Jump!" he commanded.

And she did, in a flurry of skirts and shawl, landing so hard in his arms that he staggered backward. But he was unexpectedly strong. She smiled at him, already brazening out the inevitable scold, but when their eyes met, the rest of her breath vanished, for his were blazing with laughter.

"Whittey!" Everett called sharply, and Lord Petteril dropped her feet to the ground, already reaching for his dropped sword stick.

Coming down the hill toward them, were three obvious bravos. Coming up from the other side, two more had appeared, brandishing daggers that blinded in the strong sunlight. Lope and the two bullies from inside the house spread out on either side of the door, advancing, herding Petteril, April and Everett into the middle of the narrow road. The gossiping women had vanished.

"It's a city of knife fights," Everett said ruefully. "Any good at them?"

"Not in the slightest," Petteril said. "Got any weapons?"

"A pistol, but I don't really want to fire it except as a last resort."

Between them, April took out her penknife. Petteril, no longer laughing swiped his stick viciously to fend off the brothel keepers.

"Possible breach straight ahead," said Everett. "Weak point. Fancy a charge?"

"No, but..." Petteril broke off, glancing up the hill where the sound of galloping hooves and rumbling cart wheels had caught April's attention, too.

The three bravos yelled at the African driver, who merely ploughed his large horse and cart through the middle, hurtling onward.

"Follow him," Lord Petteril yelled, grabbing April by the hand.

Using the space the horse and cart created, they flew after it—or at least hirpled as fast as they could, with April helping the badly limping captain while Petteril drew his sword from the stick, using his greater reach to fend off the pursuit.

Miraculously, the cart slowed and April helped heave Everett onto it before dashing toward Petteril. But he was right beside her. "Go!" he commanded, all but throwing her onto the cart and leaping after her.

The horse bolted forward again, galloping over the cobbles and around the corner, rattling their bones but leaving their pursuit behind. The driver turned and grinned at them.

"Well done, Dado!" April cried. She turned to Lord Petteril. "Did you recognize him?" she asked, impressed.

"No. I just crossed my fingers."

THEY ABANDONED THE cart Dado had stolen beside their original carriage, which was still waiting with its horse and the delighted children. Lord Petteril gave them another coin as they transferred to the carriage and Dado drove them gently the rest of the way to Everett's lodgings. There, the two fit men insisted on seeing Everett to his room and making sure he was none the worse for the adventure. He had blushed when April thanked him for his help, a bit like William, the footman she had met in England last month. An intriguing thought, even while she was desperate to discuss these most recent events with his lordship.

When he was back in the carriage, and she began to speak, however, he pressed her hand warningly and she began chattering about the sights instead. It wasn't difficult.

"DON'T YOU TRUST DADO?" April asked as soon as Lord Petteril had closed the door of their room. Untangling the clinging shawl from her hair and unpleasantly sweaty neck, she was certainly eager to know his lordship's opinion, but she was also striving to stave off his inevitable scold for going into the brothel.

"Right now, I don't really trust anyone," Petteril said, throwing his coat over the back of a chair and sinking into it, frowning. He stretched his long legs out in front of him—a familiar posture. "Those ruffians came out of nowhere, trapping us. They weren't just passing by. They had a mission."

"Someone sent them?" she said, considering. "Makes sense. Lope the brothel keeper could have. He certainly didn't like our questions."

"I suppose one of the women who wandered off could have summoned them. A standing order against lurking strangers like us."

"A lot of employees for a greedy pimp," April said with contempt. "But Dado saved us—it makes no sense for him to attack us."

"Dado is a pragmatist. He does what seems best at the time. Like agreeing with Lope's lie that Cartaxo had never been to the brothel when he knew better. Dado knew where we were going. He could have planned the attack in advance."

"So could Captain Everett," she retorted. "You don't suspect him."

He raised his gaze to her face. "Actually, I do. Along with anyone else who knows why we're here, who could easily have followed us."

She sat down on the sofa, dragging her fingers through her sweat-dampened hair. "Like the condessa," she said slowly. "She could definitely afford to hire men to do her dirty work. Why would she? Unless she—or her husband—killed Major Withan."

"According to Kelvin, the Cartaxos don't care for the British alliance and prefer Bonaparte's regime. Though croaking British officers and minor, if inquisitive, clerks does seem a little too blatant to be tolerated."

A knot of profound unease began to form in her stomach. "Kelvin, probably the entire Envoy's staff, know why you are here now. A clerk who never goes to the office is an oddity that must need explaining. Why would the British have croaked your cousin Bertie?"

"I doubt they would. Bertie might resent me having the title but he certainly wasn't above using the relationship to impress people."

"My cousin the viscount?" she said wryly. "Then... have they hidden him somewhere? Wouldn't that also offend his cousin the viscount?"

"Deeply," the viscount said. "Bertie seemed finally to want to be useful. I don't want that snatched from him."

"Maybe he's doing some secret work for them. Incognito," she suggested brightly, more to comfort him than because she believed it.

That raised a rueful quirk of his lips. "Bertie? A gentleman does not do the work of a lowly spy, however necessary it might be."

"These other Portuguese nobs who invited us this evening," she said, thoughtfully. "If Jeffery or Kelvin asked them to invite us, presumably they know you're here to find the major, too."

"Probably. Almeida is part of the Portuguese Regency government. He cannot be interested in a lowly British clerk without reason."

Lowly to him, she reflected, was a massive promotion to *lady* for her. "I'll put my foot in it if I go tonight. You should go without me."

His eyes, distant in thought, refocused on her. "No, you won't. We'll stick unfashionably together like the unfashionable people we are. That way you can remind me who everyone is."

He always did that. Turned things so that somehow she seemed to be doing him a favour. For no reason she could think of, a sudden lump formed in her throat. Ruthlessly, she swallowed it.

"There should be blood on the road," she said with unnecessary aggression. "Outside the brothel, if the conde died there."

Lord Petteril stirred. "There should. Probably a lot of blood if he was stabbed in the neck. And there wasn't. Wherever Cartaxo died, it was not outside the brothel."

"Someone moved his body there. Why would anyone do that? *Who* would do that?"

"Someone who wanted to discredit him. Not an honourable place to die."

April raised her eyes to his face. "Or someone who wanted to discredit your cousin. Everyone says that Major Withan went to the brothel that night."

Lord Petteril nodded slowly. "But no one admits Cartaxo did. And very probably he didn't. He died somewhere else altogether and his body was dumped there. Unless he died *inside* the brothel and they shoved his body out the window."

This was pure speculation and a little too close to April being inside the brothel, so she jumped to her feet to distract him. "There's still no blood. I'm hungry and thirsty."

"Shall we go out?"

"Yes please."

Washed, brushed and changed back into the yellow gown with a pretty, wide-brimmed straw hat to protect her indifferent complexion from the sun, she set off with him to the nearest pavement café, where they enjoyed a light luncheon, which was all April really wanted. The heat sapped her normally voracious appetite.

"Do you think he left Lisbon?" April said suddenly.

"He might have," Petteril said, grimacing. "It would be like him just to abandon his laundry. Too used to buying what he liked."

With your money, April thought resentfully. But then she too was dressed with Lord Petteril's money.

She frowned. "There must be so many British soldiers in and out of the city on leave, or for medical treatment, to say nothing of streams of new arrivals off the ships. It must be impossible to keep track of who leaves the city and when."

"Yes... But once they knew he was missing, that he was neither with his regiment nor at his lodgings in the city, why did no one trouble to look for him?"

"It's like when people die in St. Giles," April said. "It's a five minute wonder, then everyone just steps over the body and gets on with life. No one asks questions there either. Happens too often."

He met her gaze, his expression arrested. "Meaning that even with all the recent British successes like Badajoz and Salamanca, so many soldiers die out here that one more officer doesn't matter."

"Only to his family," April said gently. "And to his friends. Out here, he's not an individual gentleman, he's part of the British army."

"Like the dead bodies in St. Giles. Someone might grieve but no one else notices." He drew in his breath, then took a large mouthful of wine. "*No man is an island... any man's death diminishes me*. We should all notice."

"Is that a poem?" she asked.

"John Donne," he replied. His lips twisted. *"Never send to know for whom the bell tolls; it tolls for thee."*

April clinked her glass off his. "Nearly tolled for us."

"Why did you go in there?"

She had almost convinced herself she'd got away with it. "Because I could. And the window was shut at the top. I thought they might have locked your Bertie up there. And if they hadn't..." She swallowed some wine and pushed the glass away from her, as though it was another unpleasant memory. "Sometimes they lock girls up. Children, too."

She didn't look at him now, though she felt his gaze on her face.

"Had they?"

"No. The room was empty except for bits of old furniture. It looked and smelled like no one had been in there for years. Except the mice and rats. But whoever I was, I'd no business being up there. Someone must have heard me, knew I was snooping. I had to jump over the banister to avoid him."

"It was a jumping day."

"And a good catch on your part." She raised her eyes to his and read no anger, just frustration and anxiety, and then that vanished too, and he laughed.

"Incorrigible wretch."

She grinned at him and picked up an olive. She had grown fond of the strange taste. The passers-by were lessening as the local people retreated from the sun. In another five minutes, the awning would no longer shade them.

"We should notice," he said. "In St. Giles or anywhere else."

Not for the first time, April wished all nobs—all men—were like Lord Petteril.

Chapter Five

Duarte de Almeida lived only a few elegant streets away from the Condessa de Cartaxo, and in a very similar, classical style of house. The servants who admitted them were courteous and efficient, showing them immediately into a large, opulent salon that somehow lacked the warmth of the condessa's.

These impressions only just touched Piers. Mostly, his protective instincts were distracting him, for April, who faced down violent thugs without a qualm, was literally quaking over this social gathering.

He doubted she had any idea how beautiful she looked in her simple, silk evening gown of the deepest blue, matching her eyes almost to perfection. Although the neckline was modest, she was quite unused to revealing so much skin, and her blush of embarrassment gave a rosy glow to her normally pale skin. The modest sapphire necklace he had bought in London was clasped about her creamy throat. Her unruly golden locks were twisted into a knot behind her head, from one which one long curl dropped over her bare shoulder in a rather elegant style.

In fact. Piers had dressed her hair, threading the also-modest pearl necklace through it for greater effect. She had sat rigidly under his ministrations and then, her accent slipping only slightly, she had demanded, "Where'd you learn about women's hair?"

"One learns lots of things at Oxford," he had replied vaguely. "Admire yourself. Others will."

She hadn't believed him, of course. She was far too tense to judge.

No one understood social awkwardness better than Piers. In recent months he had learned to deal with it by playacting the haughty viscount, which he could not do here. But poor April was *all* at sea. She could never have seen such a glittering gathering of silks and jewels, except, perhaps, glimpsed through a window or, more recently, through doors. She knew there were incomprehensible differences between a viscountess and the wife of a Foreign Office clerk, but to her they were all nobs. And in this situation, he was not the top nob.

"Smile a lot and look impressed," he murmured. "And tell me if I've met anyone before..."

Her hand on his arm still shook, but at least she forced her shoulders to relax and she managed a fleeting smile which she hastily dragged back to her lips as a very elegant lady bore down upon them.

Although no longer in the first flush of youth, she possessed the kind of graceful beauty that never vanished. It merely grew with maturity and confidence. Understated and refined, she nevertheless drew the attention immediately and held it. There was something in the warmth of her smile, a conspiracy of the eyes that made one immediately her friend.

He had to remind himself that she was not necessarily his.

"Mr. Whittey," she greeted him in English, extending her elegantly gloved hand. "I am Furtunata de Almeida. How delightful that you come. And this must be your beautiful wife."

I ain't beautiful, was April's normal, scornful reply to such admiration. Fortunately, she didn't say it now, although she looked somewhat surprised as she remembered to curtsey to her hostess.

"You are too kind, Senhora," she murmured, her diction remaining perfect. "So kind of you to invite us."

"My husband and I love to meet as many of our British allies as we can. You are always welcome in our home. And here is my husband... Mr. and Mrs. Whittey, newly arrived from England," she told a darkly handsome man with a magnificent moustache.

Duarte de Almeida was not tall but made up for it by thrusting his chin upward. His greeting was that of a most hospitable host and yet he gave off a vast sense of superiority that would surely have daunted a lowly clerk. Piers decided to look meek and gratified.

"We must chat later on," the senhora said to April before gliding away to greet more guests. Piers could easily imagine Bertie pursuing her.

"Let me find you a glass of port," Almeida said, ushering Piers further into the room.

Piers patted April's hand to keep it on his arm, and obediently allowed himself to be guided. With an aimable bow, Almeida presented them both with a glass of sherry. April was obliged to let go of Piers to hold her glass.

"So how do you find our city?" Almeida asked her.

April, who had just taken a sizable mouthful of port, swallowed smoothly before replying with a smile. "It's the most beautiful place I have ever been."

"We had to rebuild it after the terrible earthquake of 1755."

"Most successfully," she said.

"You are too kind, senhora. So, Mr. Whittey." The niceties dealt with, he turned to Piers. "What precisely is your position with the British Envoy, sir?"

Since the cat was rather out of the bag there, Piers did not trouble to dissemble. "A rather nominal and temporary one with the express purpose of discovering what happened to a British officer who never reached his regiment at Cuidad Rodrigo."

"Ah, poor Major Withan." Almeida shook his head regretfully.

"You are acquainted with the major?"

"Of course. Charming fellow. Though I almost took against him for his interest in my wife!" He smiled to show that it was a joke and that he well understood such respectful interest.

"One could not fail to admire Senhora de Almeida's beauty," Piers said with perfect truth. "I do hope Major Withan did not overstep the line of propriety and offend her."

"No, no," Almeida said tolerantly. "My wife is a virtuous lady and I a jealous husband, but even I must admit that the major behaved like a perfect gentleman. He merely sighed after her like a lovesick puppy."

That sounded so unlike Bertie that Piers wondered if they were talking about the same man. Perhaps Almeida suffered from the same face-blindness as Piers.

"And how have you got on, sir?" Almeida enquired. "Have you discovered anything our own authorities have not?"

Piers's eyebrows flew up. "I had not realized the authorities, Portuguese or British, had discovered anything at all."

"And are very unlikely to," mourned Almeida. "Brigands, you know."

"You believe he is dead?"

"Sadly, yes," Almeida said with a sigh. "It is lamentably frequent outside the safety of Lisbon."

"And inside," Piers said mildly. "I hear one of your own noblemen was murdered in a back street."

It got little reaction, save an even sadder facial expression. The man's moustache might have drooped. "A terrible tragedy. What is the world coming to? I suppose we must expect more violence in a country at war."

"Then you do not subscribe to the theory I have heard hinted at, namely that Withan was responsible for the conde's death and fled punishment?"

"Oh, no, my dear fellow!" Almeida looked and sounded shocked. It might even have been genuine. "Major Withan was a gentleman, like us."

Flatterer, thought Piers, amused. Whittey might be a gentleman but he was most certainly not a nobleman of rank and political importance like Almeida.

"Might I ask when you last saw Major Withan?" Piers asked tentatively. "I am trying to trace his movements from the evening before he was due to leave the city."

"Of course. He called on us in the early evening to say farewell and to thank us for our hospitality to a stranger. It was perhaps seven of the clock."

"Did he seem well? Happy to be leaving for Spain?"

"Well, yes, and looking forward to his posting. He was very excited by our joint taking of Salamanca and the retreat of the French. He talked much of the storming of Badajoz in the spring, though it was at such terrible cost. He was eager to be part of the next battle."

Piers nodded. "That is what I have heard."

"I don't believe there is any truth, let alone evidence for any accusations you might hear about desertion. I believe he was an honourable man who fell foul of distinctly *dis*honourable bandits. I have to say—ah!" He broke off as a young lady drifted over to them. "Here is my daughter, Eliana. Eliana, Mr. and Mrs. Whittey from England, have just arrived in Portugal."

The girl was small like her father and lacked her mother's poise and beauty. In fact, she looked plain through sheer listlessness. What April would call *a drip*. On the other hand, upon introduction, a brief spark of interest did light her dull, mud-coloured eyes.

Ignoring April, she said to Piers, "Oh, you are Senhor Whittey." And then she blushed in a mottled kind of way and hastily excused herself.

Almeida muttered something below his breath, no doubt on the misfortune of two such graceful parents producing so awkward and dull an offspring. Then the smile was back. "Let me introduce you to some of my other guests..."

There followed something of a nightmare of introductions, fortunately not all at once, most to Portuguese people of great importance whom Piers had no chance of recognizing again, and not all of whom spoke much—or indeed any—English. With a few, however, he was able to discuss the war and appreciate the increased chances of allied victory in Spain this year, the French troops being so limited in numbers now by Bonaparte's ambitious invasion of Russia.

All the gentlemen of whatever age, ogled April, some flirting with their snapping dark eyes. Which was how Piers came to realize that Almeida alone had more or less ignored her.

Perhaps he really was furiously in love with his beautiful wife. Or perhaps he was only interested in what Piers knew or would believe about Bertie.

April said, "Kelvin is by the fireplace."

"I suppose it would be polite to say good evening. Point me at him, will you?"

Arm in arm once more, they approached the fireplace and the group of clearly British gentlemen all grasping their glasses of port. April rather cleverly caught Kelvin's irritable gaze and bobbed a curtsey.

"Mr. Kelvin, good evening. A pleasure to see you here."

Piers focused on the object of her attention and remembered the balding head, and the rather resentful voice that replied, "Good evening, Mrs. Whittey. Whittey. Sir Charles, I believe you are not yet acquainted with Whittey, who joined us yesterday?"

"Ah," said a tall, vaguely dissipated gentleman with the shrewd eyes. "Very glad to have you, Whittey. Mrs. Whittey, charmed." He bowed over her hand, his eyes twinkling with lazy interest.

Piers, warned by the man's charm, was not entirely surprised to be introduced to Sir Charles Stuart, British Envoy Extraordinaire to Portugal. April, to whom all nobs were equal, merely twinkled back at him.

"Come and see me next time you're in the office," Sir Charles said to Piers. "Better still, come to dinner one night and bring your delightful wife."

"The Envoy likes me," April crowed when the British huddle broke up.

"Everyone likes you. You're a likeable lady."

April laughed, a joyous enough sound to attract several long glances. "Then may I have another glass of port?"

"So long as I don't have to carry you home."

"I've been drinking spirits since I was ten years old," April said scornfully, and probably quite truthfully considering the places she had sought shelter. "It doesn't affect me."

"Yes, it does," Piers murmured after a quick glance at her glowing face. Although her radiance was as likely to be due to the success of the evening which she had not truly expected to carry off.

Unfortunately, they had not really learned anything new about Bertie, except that Piers did not trust Almeida.

"I bring you port wine," said a diffident female voice.

Piers bowed to the rather unmemorable girl before them and accepted the glass with a bow.

"Thank you, Senhorita de Almeida," April said helpfully. "This is just what I wanted."

If only I could take her to every party, Piers thought gratefully, bestowing a rather warmer smile on Eliana de Almeida.

Her eyes widened fractionally, a spark of surprise and pleasure. Then she glanced quickly around her.

"I listen to my father a little. You look for Major Withan."

"I do," Piers said in surprise. "Do you know him?"

She dropped her eyes. "A little, of course. He call here several times."

"But not after about seven o'clock on the night before he left?" April said. "Though he was certainly seen elsewhere in the city after that."

"He come at seven and say goodbye," Eliana agreed, her eyes darting again. Her voice lowered even further as embarrassment coloured her face. "He come again just after eleven, to say a more special goodbye."

"Ouch," Piers said as April pinched his arm to silence whatever else he had been about to ask.

Eliana did not appear to notice. "They all talk as if he is dead..." She glanced around her once more and let out a sound alarmingly like a sob. "We cannot talk here. I try to get away tomorrow morning, though it will be difficult. Where do you stay?"

"Latour's hotel. There is a little bakery just around the corner if you'd like to come upon us by accident."

"Eight o'clock, I come," Eliana said, and went.

"Bertie and Senhora de Almeida?" Piers said thoughtfully.

"I doubt it." April murmured. "She'd eat him for breakfast."

Piers blinked. "What a surprising little creature you are, Mrs. Whittey."

"Not at all, Mr. Whittey. Not at all."

FOR THE FIRST TIME in weeks, Eliana de Almeida glimpsed hope. Not for her happiness, but for Major Withan's life.

When her parents' reception ended and she was finally released from her obligations, she bolted to her own chamber and gazed out of the window. The summer evening was growing dark. The knot that twisted her stomach had not eased but for once she could look forward to *doing* something.

The English couple were odd, like many of the English she had encountered, and *very* odd to be important functionaries of the British government. She didn't believe for a moment that they were important. He was much too diffident and she too lively and probably air-headed, but then, she was only a wife.

That didn't matter. She could still direct them. They would be her eyes, her arms and legs in the city and beyond, to investigate and discover the truth of an investigation that no one else seemed very interested in. She herself, as an unmarried girl, was too closely chaperoned and guarded, and her parents, convinced without any evidence that the major had met his end at the hands of bandits, would do nothing to upset Portugal's Regency government or its British allies.

No one but Eliana saw anything odd about the disappearance of the British officer. Her mother had gone further.

"Why should you care? He is no one to you, and if you ever intend to be something to anyone else, you should make more effort with your appearance. Smile occasionally. Be interested in something other than the poor—you will find no husband there."

"I want no husband," Eliana had mumbled.

"How fortunate, since no husband is exactly what you will have! If your father and I do not continue to do everything for you."

Doing everything for her seemed to be entering betrothal negotiations with an ancient *barão* whom she could not recall ever meeting. And so she would move from one prison to another while nothing was done for Major Withan until he really was dead.

Her belief in his survival was not rational to anyone else. She knew that. She even knew she was willing it to be so more strongly than anyone else was imagining his death. And if he really was dead, now, she needed to know. But she refused to believe that bright, vital, impudent life had been extinguished. She would *know*, she would feel it like the darkening of the world which, without him, was universally grey and meaningless. Like the British weather he described.

She thought back to their first meeting, when, the guest of her parents, he had discovered her in the garden, hiding between the old orange tree and a nameless green bush. She had heard her parents and the servants looking for her. So had he, but instead of giving her away, he had dropped down beside her on the grass, asked what she was reading, and looked so genuinely impressed when she told him, that she had told him more. He had laughed and teased her, told her he was not remotely bookish, though he liked to read about military campaigns and strategies. And it was all said in such a way that she didn't feel inferior or ugly or mocked.

And at the reception in the evening, he had sought her out—only because of his kindness for them, her parents had told her. Eliana herself had no doubt that it was kindness. Major Withan was the most handsome man she had ever seen—dashing and reckless with those laughing eyes that refused to look seriously on the world.

He knew he was not perfect. He told her about his idle, wasted life in England, gambling and drinking and womanizing, taking advantage of his dying uncle and his absent, unworldly cousin. With the unworldly cousin's help, he had transferred to a fighting regiment under Lord Wellington and had no doubts he was doing the right thing.

Eliana was enchanted. For the first time in her life—and she was all of eighteen years old—she fell in love. Not that she had dreams. She was a realist. It was enough for her to love him. And she would not allow him to be dead.

Tomorrow. Tomorrow, she would tell the odd English couple all she knew. Branca, her maid, would give her away, of course, so she would only have this one chance.

Chapter Six

April woke with the sharp awareness of danger. Someone was moving in the almost total darkness, and that always meant trouble. She shot into a sitting position, heart pounding with fear, one arm raised over her face to ward off the worst of blows, the other searching frantically for a weapon that was not there.

The stealthy movement halted.

"April?"

Lord Petteril! Oh, thank Christ.

The bed curtain twitched, revealing pale dawn light. And no doubt allowing his lordship a glimpse of her pathetic cringe. Hastily, she dropped her arm. No wonder she could find no knife in the depths of her fine, lawn night rail.

She swallowed, licking her dry lips, recovering her orientation. "What?" she demanded aggressively. "You startled me."

"Sorry, I was trying not to wake you."

He didn't mention that her sudden, frantic movement had startled him too. She liked his concern and feared it at the same time. But she knew he would not embarrass her by mentioning her reaction.

"Where are you going?" As long as she had known him, he had risen at dawn. Even before they had been thrown so much together, she had guessed he did not sleep well. Now she knew it. He must miss his early morning rides here.

"Just for a walk. I thought I might pass by the condessa's and the Almeidas' houses."

"Great idea. I'll come with you."

"Five minutes," he said sternly. "I'll wait downstairs."

In her hurry, she splashed as much water on the floor as on her body and flung on the green walking dress she had worn to disembark from the ship, with a shawl around her shoulders to hide the erratic fastening. Ruthlessly she pinned up her hair and crammed on the straw hat, grabbed her reticule with the notebook and pencil and bolted downstairs.

Petteril was sprawling on an old sofa in the hotel foyer, reading an English newspaper that was almost two weeks old.

"Well done," he said, abandoning the paper at once, and rose to offer his arm.

From nowhere, she felt a sudden awkwardness. Perhaps because he had seen her so fearful. Perhaps because some invisible line of intimacy had been crossed. She took refuge in Mrs. Whittey, sticking her nose in the air and seizing his arm in a proprietorial fashion that made him laugh. And then, it was fine again.

They walked briskly in the cool of the dawn. April enjoyed the freshness while she could, the pleasant solitude of being up and about while the city was just beginning to wake. Only a few people were about their business already: a plodding cart horse pulling his load of milk churns, bakers stirring up their ovens.

The condessa's sleepy street was totally deserted.

"We must stick out like horns on a chicken," April muttered.

"Nonsense," Lord Petteril said. "We're British and therefore eccentric."

The house was completely shuttered. No sleepy maid emerged to scrub the front steps. No gardeners watered the flower beds before the heat of the sun emerged. April and Petteril strolled past the front gates and around the corner into the side lane.

Abruptly, Lord Petteril leapt backward, dragging her back out of the lane. Before she could protest, she glimpsed what he, with his greater height, must have seen over the wall. A man was emerging from the side gate, hastily clapping his hat onto his head and pulling it down over his nose before he hurried on down the lane, away from April and Petteril.

"Duarte de Almeida," April said in excitement. "What on earth is he doing at the condessa's house at this hour?"

"One would be naïve to ignore the obvious," Petteril murmured, drawing her onward down the main street.

"You mean Almeida is the condessa's lover?"

"Probably. But they would certainly appear to have some kind of alliance."

She stared at him. "How on earth did you guess about that?"

His lips quirked. "Actually, I didn't. I hoped we might catch some servant either here or at the Almeidas' house and learn something one can't from their masters and mistresses. Difficult when they're less likely to speak English. I wish I spoke Portuguese, or even Spanish."

April returned to the point. "Alliance. And yet she prefers the French, Almeida prefers the British."

"Does she?" Petteril wondered. "We know her husband preferred the French. I have no idea of her political views. Men discount the power of women at their peril."

"If they're allies—in whatever—she could have told him about us looking for the major. *He* could have sent those ruffians against us yesterday. They could be in it together."

"In what? Why is everyone so eager to ignore Bertie's disappearance?"

"Because they know something we don't," April said. "They know what has really happened to him."

"Does that mean he is dead or alive?" Petteril asked bleakly.

"If he was dead, would there be anything to hide?"

Petteril inclined his head. "A good point. Then where the devil is he?"

It was a rhetorical question April made no attempt to answer. By mutual if silent agreement, they avoided the Almeida house and strolled along the coast via the old monastery and some rather lovely old buildings.

Looking back at the monastery in some awe, April said, "I could believe in God in a place like that. For a little."

"I don't suppose you were ever inside St. Paul's or Westminster Abbey? I'll take you one day. And York minster."

April, who was happy to go anywhere with him, settled in the meantime for strolling the rest of the way to the bakery where they had agreed to meet Eliana de Almeida.

The patron greeted them like old friends and set places for them at the shady table under the awning, from where they could watch the increasing number of people go by, horses pulling carts and carriages, monks and nuns, singly and in groups, mingling with the wealthy and the poor of every race imaginable, all scurrying about some business or other, even just begging.

"I don't think she's coming," April said when she could cram in no more bread or pastries.

"One more cup of coffee," Piers said, signalling the baker.

In fact, Eliana appeared while he was pouring it. A crested carriage ambled past in the road. A veiled lady suddenly pulled down the window and called something about English friends, April thought, then issued an order to the coachman.

Another voice sounded, protesting and outraged, but the carriage halted and the veiled lady jumped down quite unaided. An older woman, stiff with outrage, began to follow. The younger, turned, impatiently waving her away with sharp instructions.

The young lady, hurried toward April and Petteril, while the older slammed the carriage door to assuage her temper and the carriage moved off.

Lord Petteril stood up, and the lady pushed back her veil to reveal Eliana, not listless in the slightest, her whole face alight with determination. She acknowledged his lordship's bow with an impatient nod and sat down in the seat he held for her. Pulling up another, Petteril asked for coffee for the lady.

"We must be quick," Eliana said briskly. "I have probably only a quarter hour before the carriage comes back for me. You look for Major Withan, but there are many things you do not know. He is not a stupid man. He would not travel alone through unknown bandit country. He would not die quietly, or even be taken quietly for ransom—a ransom that is never asked."

Again, Petteril inclined his head.

"What do you know?" April asked bluntly.

"I know he did not fight a duel with the late Conde de Cartaxo."

"If that happened," Petteril said, "it did so after ten o'clock when he left—er... a house in the poorer district of the city."

"I see him after eleven and he fight no duel. My parents believe Cartaxo challenge him for—hmmm..." She struggled for the words.

"Being the condessa's lover?" April supplied.

"*Sim,*" Eliana said gratefully, with no sign of embarrassment. "Which he never was."

"With respect, senhorita," Petteril said, when more coffee had been brought, "how do you know that?"

"He tell me." A hint of a blush stained her cheeks.

Curiously, this time it did not mottle her skin unattractively but lent her a rosy glow. She would never be pretty, but she had her own form of beauty that stemmed perhaps from her inner kindness and intelligence. April liked her. She was sure Bertie Withan did not deserve her.

Eliana said in a rush. "That night, he come back after eleven, secretly, to say a private farewell to me."

Petteril's gaze never left her face. "To you?" he said carefully.

"We are friends." Eliana's chin lifted. "So I know women like the condessa..." She seized a breath. "Like my mother, they bore him."

Petteril frowned. "Senhorita, did my—did the major offer you marriage?"

Eliana shook her head. "He never marry someone like me. But he *sees* me. He likes me." Involuntarily, it seemed her gloved hand came up and touched her lips, then fell hastily back into her lap. "I cannot make you understand. It does not matter. But you must look for him. That same night, he discovered something about Cartaxo. You know the conde thrive under Bonaparte's regime? He pledges loyalty to the Regent's government, and the French are pushed out, but Major Withan believes Cartaxo is still an enemy."

"Why?"

Eliana shook her head in frustration. "I do not know. He would not tell me—for my safety. But the major is not a discreet man."

"No," Petteril agreed fervently.

"His disappearance is something to do with Cartaxo," Eliana insisted. "And not the affaire with his wife, which never happen."

Petteril, idly stirring his coffee while he gazed at her, said, "What do you think happened to the major, senhorita? Where do you think he is?"

Eliana leaned forward, speaking urgently now. "I think the condessa have him. Imprisoned."

Petteril blinked. "In her house?"

"One of her houses," Eliana said impatiently. "Not in Lisbon—too difficult, too busy. But there is a country house outside the city, near the aqueduct..." She opened her reticule and snatched out a piece of paper which she thrust at April. "Here is the address. No one will wonder if you go and admire the aqueduct. Most visitors do. Also, there is a warehouse in the city, owned by Cartaxo. I don't know what other properties he had. Major Withan could be in any of them, but I think it would be difficult to move him too far away. Perhaps I just hope. Mr. Whittey, you will keep looking for him?"

Petteril continued to meet her anxious gaze, deep in thought.

"He will," April said.

Eliana glanced at her and smiled. "Thank you. And be careful who you trust." She uttered something below her breath. "And here is my carriage."

"Why rush?" April said. "You are a lady. You may keep the servants waiting while you finish your coffee. They are insolent to expect otherwise."

Petteril blinked at her.

Eliana laughed. "I like you. You marry a kind man. Was he your choice?"

Now it was April's turn to blush a rather fiery red, but she could only say, "Yes, of course." She pulled herself together. "Will your parents not let you choose?"

Eliana wrinkled her nose. "Only if he is a rich old baron more than forty years old. Perhaps I become a nun."

"Don't do it before we find Major Withan," April said hastily.

Eliana smiled, finished her coffee and rose to her feet. Petteril and April rose with her, bowed and curtseyed and they parted with perfect propriety.

As the carriage drew away again, Petteril rummaged distractedly for some coins to pay the bill.

He was silent as they began to walk back to the hotel. Then he said abruptly, "If Bertie has led that girl on, I may never forgive him."

"I don't know that he has," April said. "Do you really think he could fool her?"

Lord Petteril opened his mouth, then closed it again in further silence, looking thoughtful. "You think then that the flowers he bought that night were for her? Not for her mother or the condessa?"

"Probably. Dado didn't say what time he bought them."

"No, he made it sound as if it was early in the evening, Or, at least, that's what I took from what he said. But the condessa said Bertie wore no flower when he called on her and the conde. Dado must have seen him buy them later. After he had been to the Cartaxos, the Almeidas for the first time, and the bordello, but before he returned to see Eliana. Unless he lied to her and was really there to see her mother, just ran into Eliana by accident."

"My money's on Eliana. And he doesn't deserve her."

"Look on the bright side, he's very unlikely to get her if her choices are the old baron or the nunnery."

They fell silent, each mulling the matter over.

"If we can find a map," he said at last, "shall we ride out and admire this aqueduct?"

"And the condessa's country house?"

"It would be a shame to miss it."

However, walking into the hotel, his lordship was presented with an urgent note from Jeffery in the Envoy's office.

Petteril raised his eyes slowly to April's. His face betrayed a mixture of jubilation, doubt and anxiety. "They have a ransom demand."

TWENTY MINUTES LATER, Piers faced Jonathan Jeffery across a desk, this time in a private office with the door closed.

Piers let the ransom letter fall to the desk and took off his spectacles. "Who knows about this?"

"Just you and me. And Sir Charles, of course."

"And whichever lowly clerk opened his post."

Jeffery shook his head. "No, it was addressed for the private attention of Sir Charles. I left it on his desk. It was he who summoned me. He wanted to meet you himself but in the end, we decided it was more discreet if I speak to you alone."

Piers shifted in his seat. "You do not trust the staff here?"

"I wouldn't say that," Jeffery protested. He hesitated, then, "Diplomatic missions can be a little complicated. Naturally, our goal is the same, but we differ as to how to achieve it, and how to build our petty little empires to ensure we get the individual credit."

"I met Kelvin with Sir Charles at Senhor de Almeida's house last night."

"Kelvin believes Almeida best serves the interests of the King in Portugal."

"Does he?"

"He serves his own country first and no doubt his own family before that. We are none of us so very different."

Piers looked him in the eye. "Did you know Almeida is having a liaison of some kind with the Condessa de Cartaxo?"

Jeffery's eyes widened. "No," he said slowly. "That, I did not know. And you have only been here five minutes."

"Two days, and I am rather more free to go where I like when I like."

"Does it have bearing on this?" Jeffery waved one hand at the ransom note.

"I don't know," Piers admitted. "But the timing is damned strange. Why demand a ransom now? If Withan is being held somewhere, why wait weeks to issue this?"

"Perhaps they didn't understand his value before you appeared in the city asking questions."

"Possible," Piers admitted. Putting on his spectacles once more, he picked up the note. "But then why hold him so long?"

"You think they don't have him at all? Are merely chancing their arms for a little free loot?"

"It crossed my mind."

"It is written in poor English," Jeffery said. "Like a foreigner's best effort. The hand is ill-formed."

"It could just as easily be someone *pretending* to have poor English, and anyone can disguise their handwriting." To prove it, he picked up a pen and a blank piece of paper from Jeffery's side of the desk and wrote a perfect copy of the first two lines of the note.

Jeffery closed his mouth. "I won't ask where you learned that."

"Schoolboy trick. Much in demand from my fellow pupils. I earned a lot of tuck. If my presence is the catalyst for this demand, it has to be someone who knows why I am here. They want us to leave the ransom in the Church of Santa Cruz at midnight and say they will then release Major Withan. They don't say where they will release him... How was the note delivered?"

Jeffery shrugged. "We don't know. No one remembers any personal deliveries but it was with the rest of the post when I got in this morning." He paled. "You don't think someone here is involved, do you?"

"It's possible," Piers retorted, "and you think so too or we wouldn't be shut away here instead of shouting this outrage to the world. What would happen if you told the Portuguese authorities?"

"They'd probably execute some villain to keep us happy, whether he is guilty or not."

"Hmmm. If these people have Withan, and we pay, they will either just kill him or try to get us to pay again. If they don't have him, we're paying for nothing and are no farther forward."

"It is not our policy to pay ransoms," Jeffery said quietly. "It encourages the practise of kidnap. Privately, I believe the Envoy would pay to see Withan returned to us. He knows the family."

"So I believe." He drummed his fingers on the desk. "As it happens, the family has given me access to sufficient funds. If we choose to go down that road."

"You do not have long to decide. I can find a few soldiers to protect you, unofficially—"

"I think that might draw too much attention. The money is to be left under the seat of the far-left back pew of the church, and then we must scarper. Presumably, the perpetrator will be watching. Sir, do the Almeida family own a country house near Lisbon?"

Jeffery's eyes widened. "I don't believe so. Their land is all to the north."

"What of property within the city? I believe the Cartaxos own at least one warehouse here. Do the Almeidas have something similar? Other business interests?"

"Some, I suspect, but—"

Piers stood and held the ransom note under the light. He could just make out a water mark. Not such cheap paper after all, just rubbed to make it appear so. He stuffed it in his pocket.

"Could you send me any details you can easily and discreetly learn? We're still at Latour's."

"Whittey, I have enough to do!" Jeffery said in annoyance. "This task is yours."

Piers blinked at him behind his blurry reading glasses and smiled sheepishly. "I know, but I promised to take my wife to see the Áquaduto das Aguas Livres."

PIERS RETURNED TO THE hotel with two fully saddled horses which Dado was delighted to look after for him while he went to fetch April.

"You ride outside the city?" he asked eagerly. "I take you?"

"Not this time," Piers said with a grin. "I'm not long married, you know. Barely married at all!"

He found April dressed in her new riding habit, though unable to fasten the hooks at the back, a husbandly duty he focused on quite hard. Her skin always smelled so sweet and fresh. She stood stiffly before him, enduring.

He dropped his hands. "Ready? I brought horses back with me and I have a map."

"So have I," she crowed. Her face was alight with the anticipation of pleasure, for she loved horses and had enjoyed her riding lessons at Haybury Court. "What happened with the Envoy?"

"I'll tell you as we go. We have a lot to do today."

Chapter Seven

The towering aqueduct which carried Lisbon's water supply across miles of difficult country was certainly spectacular, especially the massive arches across a charming valley.

April and Lord Petteril rode down into the valley, halting their horses to marvel.

"Just imagine the carnage if it collapsed," April said.

"It survived the earthquake, so I doubt there's much that can harm it."

April was dubious and glad not to be too close. As far as she could tell, they had not been followed, though there were a few fellow admirers of the aqueduct in sight, including a couple of British soldiers, presumably on leave. The sudden appearance of those ruffians outside the brothel bothered her, and she scanned both ridges of the valley for signs of anyone with a rifle.

She found she was glad when they rode up the other side of the valley and had a better view of the surrounding country. Following the map, they rode away from the viaduct toward the Cartaxo country house.

In fact, it was not easy to find. There seemed to be no road to speak of, and the first tracks they followed led to rather squalid little farms. At the second of those, Lord Petteril gave up on discretion. When a rather vacant woman emerged from her hovel, he asked, "Casa de Conde de Cartaxo?"

The woman didn't speak, merely pointed behind her toward the woods and went back into the house, no doubt because a baby was crying.

"Actually, this is quite hopeful," April said, urging her placid mount on. "The house must be ideal to hide someone—isolated and difficult to find."

"I wouldn't like to take a carriage through here."

The woods gave April the shivers, not least because she and his lordship had once found a corpse in just such a place. And besides, anyone could be skulking behind all those trees. Still, at least they were shaded from the ferocious sun.

At last, they saw a glimmering of a building through the trees and pressed on with excitement. They emerged from the wood into what had once been a formal, walled garden. Much of the wall had fallen or been knocked down, creating breaches through which they led their horses. The house itself was at the end of a wildly overgrown path, with a front terrace and what might once have been a drive leading in the opposite direction.

"We should go that way when we leave," April said. "We must have missed the road and come too far. Do you think there's anyone here?"

"Doesn't look like it."

The house was shuttered and blank, its impressive oak front doors resembling a castle's. Lord Petteril used the huge, gargoyle-like knocker to thunderous effect, while April meandered toward the drive and peered through the trees lining what might once have been a gracious avenue.

Somewhere toward the foot was another, much smaller building, like a lodge house. And someone was definitely moving there, hanging laundry, she thought.

She hurried back to Petteril, telling him what she had seen. He was trying the door, which was definitely locked, if not bolted on the inside.

"I suppose we'd better go to the lodge then," Petteril said. "Though I'm not sure that being English and nosey will be a good enough excuse to get us into the main house. But they might know something or give something away."

"They might," April agreed, eyeing the large front door and its massive keyhole with disfavour. "But we might as well have a look here first. A back door would be easier."

He cast her a sardonic glance and resorted to thieves' cant. "On the dub lay again, April?"

She didn't dignify that with a response, merely handed the reins of her horse to Petteril, who tied them in the shade of a useful tree at the back of the house, while April extracted her lock picking tools from her reticule and set about unlocking the back door.

It took her an annoying amount of time, but it gave eventually—fortunately not bolted. Presumably, the people at the lodge kept an eye on the place and entered and left by this door.

"I suppose I shouldn't congratulate you on such a dubious talent," his lordship murmured, "but well done."

She tried not to preen. They both paused at the entrance, listening intently.

"The place feels empty," he said without expression, yet she still felt his disappointment.

"We only know that it's quiet," she argued. "It's a big house."

"It is." Gently, he pulled her aside, obviously meaning to brush past her into the house, but she resisted.

"I'll go in," she said. "I can get into any locked rooms and I can hide more easily. You be my watchman and give me warning if anyone's coming."

"April, if Bertie's in there, chances are, so is a guard or two."

"Then I'll come and tell you. I'm used to creeping about in dark kens."

"Mind your cant," he said mechanically, chewing a corner of his lip in indecision. Then unexpectedly he threw his head back and made a horrible noise alarmingly like a crow. "If you hear that, you get out. And if you're not out in ten minutes, I'm coming in. Take no chances, April, I mean it."

She nodded agreement, trying to look impatient when she was actually secretly touched by his care. Again. Reluctantly, he got out of her way, and she went inside.

The kitchen was large, clean but unused. The stove was stone cold and empty. Grimacing she went on her way, checking the servants' quarters for signs of occupancy and finding only stripped beds in a small dormitory.

In the main house, most of the doors were open. She walked noiselessly on tiled floors through opulent halls that smelled musty although there were no obvious cobwebs until she approached the stairs. Her neck prickled, expecting a heavy hand on her shoulder, the sudden leap of attack. She took a deep breath and crept upward.

One bedchamber was made up, as if for any unexpected visitor, but again the room smelled musty and unused. It had not been aired for months if not years.

A creaking floorboard froze her to the spot. She waited, listening desperately over the thundering beat of her heart.

Nothing happened. She crept behind the door, peering through the narrow gap caused by the hinges, and then, even more warily around the door into the passage. Again, she waited for the attack as she left the room and then glanced into the next and the next. Although she longed to find Bertie Withan for his lordship's sake, she found herself perversely glad the house betrayed no signs of life.

It was the attic she feared the most. Old tales and legends combined with her own experience of rookeries with vicious traps and equally vicious humans behind them. But she forced herself to go up there, too. Part of it was a storeroom, like at Haybury Court, Lord Petteril's main seat. Through another door, which needed the services of her trusty lockpicks, she found another servants' dormitory, also bare and unused.

Deflated, she paused in the doorway, wondering if there was anywhere she had missed, when the call of a crow had her jumping out of her skin.

She bolted, half falling down the dark servants' stairs for speed, ignoring the clattering of her footsteps and the thud of things she bumped into in the passage past the kitchens. Only there did she adjust her speed and stealth, creeping to the back door.

Lord Petteril stood outside, holding the reins of both horses, who were nudging each other in competition for a bucket of water.

"Who's coming?" April panted, annoyed by this nonchalance.

"No one. Your time was up."

April growled at the back of her throat and snatched at the reins of her horse. "No sign that anyone's been there for months. Years probably. Someone cleans the downstairs rooms and one bedchamber, but it's never been aired."

"We had to check," Petteril said ruefully. "And there is still the lodge."

Accordingly, they walked down the driveway. A glowering man emerged from the cottage and Lord Petteril, with his most amiable and vague smile, informed him in a mixture of mime and spoken English peppered with the odd word of Portuguese that they had come upon the house from the woods, and no one appeared to be home.

The glowering man's suspicions appeared to be only slightly calmed, and his wife came out to inspect them, too. April, peering through the front door, saw that the cottage appeared to be one large room in a single floor with only one tiny window. If they were hiding anyone in there, he was standing very co-operatively behind the door.

"Barking up the wrong tree," Lord Petteril said when he had boosted her into the saddle and they began their return journey.

"We still have the warehouse Eliana wrote down," April reminded him.

"And hopefully Jeffery will come up with a few more."

Returning to Lisbon in the full heat of the sun, April began to appreciate the local custom of the afternoon *sesta*, when many shops closed and work stopped until the marginally cooler evenings.

Back at the hotel, they found Dado dozing in the shade at the corner. Petteril paid him to return the horses to their livery stable, and they went inside. Again, his lordship was presented with a sealed packet which he didn't open until they were in the privacy of their own room.

He scanned it quickly. "From Jeffery. Almeida seems to have many business interests. Made a fortune with shipping. He has several warehouses on the docks too." He glanced up at her frowning. "I can go alone, if you're tired. I doubt there's any need for both of us. Odd to see a lady there in fact."

"Then they might lower their guards in astonishment. I'll just change first though."

"Me too," Petteril said, beating a hasty retreat to his dressing room.

The luke-warm water in the washing jug was at least refreshing, though April wished she could go out in her shift. Reluctantly, she pulled the blue gown back on, contorting herself to fasten her own hooks before Petteril emerged again, perhaps wearing a clean shirt and necktie but otherwise looking exactly the same.

"To the docks, Mrs. Whittey?"

"To the docks," she agreed. "Um...we might be quicker with Dado to guide us."

"I was just thinking that."

"Then you trust him again?"

"Not necessarily, but we're giving him no time to summon any bravos. If they're waiting for us, the finger will point directly to Jeffery."

Dado was delighted to act as guide and took them first to the address given by Eliana. Although the docks themselves were still bustling, the warehouses behind seemed to be largely deserted. So Petteril stood on Dado's proffered back to peer in the window, wobbling precariously before he jumped down.

"Totally empty," he said, from which April gathered there was nowhere to hide or be hidden either.

Dado shrugged, rubbing his shoulders. "Most trade only with the army now. Less silks and spices. Many people lose money."

Petteril's gaze flew to his. "Good point," he said slowly.

"Why?" April murmured as they marched off to the first on Jeffery's list.

"I don't know," his lordship said. "A germ of an idea that won't quite form."

It was an exhausting couple of hours, tramping long, flat distances, occasionally facing sullen watchmen, sometimes climbing on each other to see in barred windows while the third person kept watch.

"Almost like the old days," April murmured.

His lordship glanced at her askance and bumped his knee against a crate abandoned outside a warehouse door. Since they were en route to Almeida's last known place of business, and had little hope left, April wasn't terribly interested. This warehouse was not on their list.

"Ouch." Petteril bent to rub his knee. The lid of the crate must have been loose, for it had shifted. Petteril reached inside and half pulled up a dumpy bottle which he hastily dropped again when someone shouted from the warehouse door. "So sorry," Petteril said in amiable English. "I tripped over it. Have I damaged anything?"

There followed a torrent of angry Portuguese which Dado translated diplomatically as "No you have not."

The warehouseman slammed and locked the door and picked up the crate before walking off with it to a cart already piled with various other crates and bundles.

"I don't suppose this belongs to Senhor de Almeida?" Petteril murmured, consulting his list with the aid of the quizzing glass back around his neck.

"No," said Dado. "The late Conde de Cartaxo. So I suppose it is the condessa's now."

"Is it, by God?" Petteril said and promptly veered around the corner of the building. There was one small window at the back, relatively low down, so he bent and spread his joined hands for April to step up and peer in.

"Mostly empty," she reported. "Apart from a few crates like that one. And shelves of what looks like medical supplies—bottles of medicines, sheets and bandages and knives and such. And nowhere to hide."

Petteril sighed and lowered his hands again to let her step down. "Damn. Very well. Last one, and then back to the hotel."

The last one seemed to have been an office building, completely shut up and empty.

They trudged wearily back to the hotel and Petteril paid Dado for his time.

SINCE DUSK WAS BEGINNING to fall, Lord Petteril sent for some food, then sat on the balcony, legs stretched out while he thought.

He thought a lot, did Lord Petteril. When she had first met him, this had fascinated April, who had never had much leisure to think of anything but the next few hours survival—food, safety, who and where to avoid. Her dreams had always been brief and fantastical, like earning enough from her thieving partner to get out of St. Giles and find a real job and a room of her own where she could lock the door at night.

In England, with Lord Petteril, she had all those things. Sometimes she still couldn't believe her luck. Even though his lordship was the one person she never wanted to lock out.

On the other hand, this adventure to Portugal, begun so light-heartedly on her part at least, was growing dangerous. They had run out of options. She knew Petteril would pay the ransom. He could easily be killed during that payment, and even if he was not, Bertie Withan would die, and Petteril would always blame himself. That old cow, his aunt, the Dowager Lady Petteril, would blame him too.

Stepping over his lordship's legs, she sat on the stool beside him and gazed out at the pleasantly foreign scene below them. The town was awake again, now that the sun was down. Dusk was short here, and there was danger and tragedy to come. But if April had learned anything in her life it was to live in the moment. And these moments were peaceful and companionable, and she wouldn't have had them any other way.

Petteril drew in his legs and she knew he was about to stand up.

"You're going to pay," she blurted.

"Yes."

She met his gaze. "You know if they have him, they'll kill him to stop him identifying them."

His lips quirked. "Yes. But I have a plan."

THE CHURCH OF SANTA Cruz was within the walls of the old castle town built in medieval times by the Moors.

"There used to be a mosque there," his lordship told her as they walked up the hill past the cathedral known as the Se, and on toward the castle. It was after eleven at night, but outside lanterns and torches still lit the way. "When they drove the Moors out, the Portuguese built a church there instead, though I think it was largely rebuilt again after the earthquake. The Moors that were left were all confined to nearby Mouraria."

Although part of her mind found this interesting, most of it was occupied with possible threats. Her throat was dry, and within her dark cloak, her hand was barely an inch from the little dagger she had hung from her belt. He had refused to take Dado or Everett or anyone from the Envoy's office, so it was up to her to protect him.

The fact that he made no fuss about her accompanying him told her that he believed the danger was minimal. He was wrong. He didn't know these kinds of people as she did, men—and women—who'd slit your throat for a pocket handkerchief, let alone a bag of gold. People who might already have been to gaol and had no intention of ever going back. To them, life was cheap, especially someone else's.

So Petteril talked desultorily, and April watched like a hawk, observing everyone who passed, everyone above and below. He was quieter as they entered the village-like area of Santa Cruz.

As agreed, April fell behind, trying to look like a solitary, grieving widow. A coffee house was still open. Covertly, April regarded the few men sitting there and recognized none of them.

The church dominated the square, although it was not nearly as large as the Se, or the church they had seen at Belem. By the watch Lord Petteril had hung around her neck, the time was almost midnight.

She walked up to the church and pushed open the door. The light within surprised her, much of it coming from a mass of candles lit before the altar at the front.

She paused, searching the pews and the dark corners for signs of life, while pretending to admire the gilded alcoves and side chapels. There were many doors. Above one, as the helpful hotel maid had informed her, was a small, carved wooden balcony—a pulpit? Certainly, an important part of their plan.

As far as she could tell, there was no one around to see, but she walked up the central isle, bowed and crossed herself as Petteril had taught her, then sat in the front pew and bowed her head over her clasped hands. She slipped down onto her knees.

A few moments later, the church door creaked open again behind her. Every hair stood up on the back of her neck, but she did not turn at once to see if it was Petteril. Instead she forced herself to wait a few seconds. No footsteps approached up the aisle. She rose, put a coin in the box and lit a candle. She wasn't quite sure of the significance, but she did it anyway. Her hands didn't even shake.

Then she stepped back, crossed herself once more and walked back down the aisle. In the back pew sat a figure she did not look at. *It had better be you.*

She left the church to find the "village" just as it had been. She walked away around the street to the side. No one followed her. With luck, no watchers would be interested in her, but in Petteril with his bag of money under the seat.

Seeing no one else about, she opened the gate back into the little church yard and walked around the building until she found the side door to the vestry. This was locked as expected, so she got to work with her lock picks, which had proved their worth already that day.

She just hoped the door was not bolted on the inside. Why should it be? There must be times the priest would want to enter quietly...

The lock opened and she almost stumbled inside into total darkness and closed the door behind her. Rather than blunder about and make a racket – there was no guarantee she was the only person in the church – she knelt down on the floor and took the candle and flint from her bag. Praying she didn't set the church on fire through blindness, she struck sparks until the candle was lit.

She grasped it and rose, peering along the passage by its small glow, raising it to right and left as she went. It seemed to go on forever. But at last she found the narrow spiral stairs.

This was where she was meant to wait for Lord Petteril. Because whoever was awaiting the ransom could easily be up there hiding already. She couldn't hear movement or smell anyone.

Best get it over. She set her foot on the first step just as the side door to the church pushed softly open, and her heart leapt. Petteril? Or the collector of the ransom? Or the priest come to see who had invaded his inner sanctum...

The dark figure moved toward her, and she knew, even before the candle light flickered over his face, that it was his lordship. No one else moved with quite that loose-limbed lope, more like the dangerous, watchful clerk he had sometimes played than the haughty strut of the viscount...

"April," he breathed, blinking in the candlelight.

She grinned, still relieved and started to climb. The staircase was short, only a few tightly curling steps and then a heavy curtain which she nearly set on fire with her candle. Hastily, she blew out the candle, rubbed the curtain between her fingers to make sure it wasn't about to burn.

Petteril's hand closed on her shoulder, pulling her back, so he could enter first. The curtain moved, revealing the faint glow from the church. He nodded once, and they both crouched and crawled into the pulpit.

No one below would see them here. She sat with her back against the wood, Petteril beside her with his knees drawn up.

The church was open all night to the faithful. Anyone could come in, but nobody did. No one moved below or made a sound.

"I didn't see anyone watching us," April breathed.

"Neither did I. I left the money and saw no one else enter the church as I walked around to the vestry entrance."

"Whoever it is, is very careful," April said, not without fear. "Too good at this for my liking." She rose and peered down at the empty pews. Under the one at the back, at the far left where she had glimpsed Petteril earlier, she imagined the shadow of the money bag.

She sat back down to wait. The door would creak obligingly when anyone came in. She drew her shawl back from her hair and wrapped the cloak more closely around her—*why are churches always so cold?*—and rested her head against the wood. Beside her, Lord Petteril stretched out his long legs. They weren't quite touching but she was grateful for his nearness, his warmth. It was curiously comforting.

She closed her eyes, just for a minute.

Chapter Eight

Piers woke with hair tickling his cheek and the rare warmth of a soft, female body against his side, her head on his chest. She smelled of April, which confused him in many ways until he realized it *was* April and that his rear was numb from sitting on the hard wooden floor in the Church of Santa Cruz.

No one had entered to collect the ransom, and they had both fallen asleep. Her head must have dropped onto his shoulder, while his cheek now rested against her hair. It was sweet, and just a little heady. Her trust made him ache with pride and all the secret feelings he had vowed never to think about.

Instead of drawing back, he let the moment linger too long, for it must have been instinct that woke him. The church door creaked open, beginning to echo.

Very gently, Piers touched one finger to her lips. Her eyes flew open at once, staring into his. For an instant, he imagined they melted into impossible warmth. Her lips quirked into a smile that froze as she became aware of the opening door below.

He removed his finger. They drew apart. The church door closed again on silence.

It was no longer quite dark. Early dawn light seeped through the church windows, adding to that of the few candles still burning. Birds had begun to sing on the roof.

Footsteps sounded below, quick and confident, not coming to bow to Jesus on the cross, but moving across the back of the church. April's eyes widened, staring at Piers in hope, then in triumph as they heard the sound of rummaging, a grunt of satisfaction.

As the footsteps sounded again, Piers and April moved as one, peering over the top of their balcony. A surprisingly well-dressed man strode behind the pews toward the doors. His own lantern shone clearly on his face. If only Piers could recognize it.

The door creaked and slammed behind him, and Piers sprang to his feet, bolting through the curtain and sliding most of the way down the curving steps to the passage below.

April was right behind him. He didn't even need to ask.

"Almeida," she said with satisfaction.

DUARTE DE ALMEIDA COULD not help his small crow of satisfaction as his hand closed around the jingling bag of money. Somehow, he had thought it would be bigger, but this was certainly easier to hide. He stuffed it into his document bag, seized his lantern and marched out of the church, smiling.

Really, this was too easy. Why had he not thought of it before? Well, it was not something to do too often. Only in emergencies.

He strode across the square and along the winding street to where he had made his carriage wait.

"Home," he said cheerfully to his coachman and climbed in.

He could not wait to examine his treasure. Even before the horses moved, he had opened the document case and pulled out the bag of coins. Lovely gold coins, he saw with satisfaction, and he yanked the drawstrings and plunged his fingers in. They closed around a slip of paper.

Frowning—there really weren't that many coins and surely they were too small—he pulled out the paper. Scrawled in capital letters in English were the words: *A QUARTER NOW, THE REST UPON THE RELEASE, SAFE AND WELL, OF MAJOR WITHAN.*

Almeida hurled the bag onto the seat beside him and cursed fluently. He was so angry he didn't even notice that the carriage still had not moved. He had just realized his coachman was talking to someone when the carriage door flew open and two people leapt inside, plonking themselves on the seats opposite without as much as a "by your leave."

The horses moved forward at last. Stunned, Almeida blinked at his panting, uninvited passengers.

Blessed Virgin, it was that English fool Whittey and his really rather charming wife.

"Do let me drop you off somewhere," Almeida said with heavy sarcasm. Really, the English were so damned rude.

"Certainly," Whittey replied, watching as Almeida casually swept a couple of fallen coins back into the bag and returned it to his document case. "Take us, if you please, to Major Withan."

Almeida's jaw dropped. There seemed to be nothing he could do about that. The blood sang in his ears as his perfect plot began to crumble.

"Withan? Withan?" he gibbered. "How should I know about—"

"Senhor, please," Mrs. Whittey interrupted, leaning forward. "We saw you collect the ransom and followed you. Your game is up, and you now have only two choices."

"A man may go to church!" Almeida blustered. "If you refer to this money, I found it under the seat and fully intend to give it to the Bishop of—"

"Senhor," Whittey said wearily.

Almeida glared at him, flaring his nostrils in his haughtiest manner as his full, justified confidence returned. Who did this jumped up clerk think he was? Almeida merely had to snap his fingers in the presence of Sir Charles Stuart, the British Envoy Extraordinaire, and Whittey would be on the first ship home, demoted if not dismissed. His story would never be believed.

And yet Whittey's gaze did not drop before his. Those weak, diffident eyes were suddenly neither. The man was not remotely afraid. *His* presence, not Almeida's, dominated the carriage. *His* voice lashed Almeida with contempt.

"I believe my wife was pointing out your remaining choices. And you will listen. Proceed, my dear."

"By all means," said Mrs. Whittey, her pretty face strangely authoritative, even if she lacked the dignity of his own wife Fortunata.

Oh, God, Fortunata... If this came out... Of course it would not. Sir Charles.

"Your first choice," Mrs. Whittey pursued, "is to come with us to the Envoy's office, where your coachman is currently driving us and where you will be formally accused and handed over to the Portuguese authorities. I should advise you that my husband is following the orders of the Envoy himself and that I very much doubt your own people will look favourably on your independent little venture."

It is over, he thought numbly. *Everything is over. Or is it?* "And my other choice?" He hated the hoarseness in his own voice, especially before the scornful Englishman looking down his nose as if he had every right.

"The second?" Mrs. Whittey said. "Why, that you take us immediately, as first requested, to Major Withan and release him to us. Depending on his state, you may then keep your booty, and no formal charges will be brought against you."

Whittey stirred. "Naturally, I cannot control diplomatic chatter. I cannot swear your career will not founder. But at least you will not spend your life in prison or end it on the rope. Probably." He glanced casually out of the window. The sun was rising. "You may give your coachman fresh instructions if you wish."

Not by the faintest twitch did Whittey betray tension. He even had his hands shoved into his pockets. Almeida might have imagined he was bored had those damned, steely eyes not remained so steady as though reading and despising Almeida's every thought.

"I cannot," Almeida whispered. He didn't mean to say the words but as soon as they were out, he realized they were true. "You are wrong. I have no choice. I cannot face the shame of arrest. Nor can I tell you where to find Major Withan."

Whittey's lips curved into a very unpleasant smile that chilled Almeida's blood.

Mrs. Whittey said in amused astonishment. "You are afraid of *them*? My dear senhor, I think you do not quite know my husband and me well enough. Yet."

Almeida shivered and closed his eyes to blot them both out. "You do not understand. I would tell you if I could. I cannot because I do not know."

There was complete silence in the carriage. Even the rumble of wheels and the clop of hooves seemed oddly muffled. Forcing open his eyes, he saw the couple exchange glances.

"You do not know," Whittey repeated.

Miserably, Almeida shook his head. "I wrote the ransom demand. I had a beggar deliver it to the Envoy's office. But I never had the major."

"Never?"

"The last time I saw him was as I told you, at seven o'clock when he came to bid my wife and I farewell. I heard he was missing, of course, but to be frank I never thought of him again until you began sniffing around and asking questions."

"And you are short of funds," Whittey said, throwing back his head against the squabs with something like frustration. "Business is poor. The war has not helped you."

"You know no such thing," Almeida said, even now attempting dignity and pride.

"Yes, I do," said the hateful Whittey. "Your offices and your warehouses are empty. Your daughter's day gown has been darned, her shoes re-heeled and soled. You are desperate to marry her to a rich man before your poverty becomes common knowledge and you are angry that she is no femme fatale like your beautiful wife."

The blood which seemed to have all drained away from Almeida's face now rushed back into it, making him dizzy and hot. "How dare you?" he gasped.

"Keep your hair on," said Mrs. Whittey inexplicably. "Don't have an apoplexy. Your one hope is to tell us everything."

Almeida slumped. "I already have. I know no more."

"Tell me," Whittey said thoughtfully, "was the Conde de Cartaxo in such straights as you?"

"No, damn him, he was selling arms and medical supplies to the French and the Portuguese, and then to the British, too."

"Does the Portuguese government know that?"

Almeida shrugged. "It is an open secret. One of the warehouses was raided in retaliation."

"Did you put the Portuguese up to that?" Mrs. Whittey enquired.

Sensing an opportunity to ingratiate himself with those who held his life in their hands, Almeida smiled modestly. "I might have."

"Striking down a rival," Whittey murmured. "And yet I think it backfired, because now Cartaxo's widow does not have so much blunt at the ready. Did you mean to elope with her using the ransom?"

Almeida groaned and closed his eyes again, utterly humiliated. "She won't. And yet neither will she break it off. You have been in Lisbon three days. How can you know *everything*?"

"I don't know where Major Withan is," Whittey said bleakly.

Almeida forced some pity into his face and voice. He even felt a little. "He is dead. Somewhere between Lisbon and Cuidad Rodrigo. Many are dead and missing. Why do you try so hard for this one? Because his cousin is an important man?"

"Yes," said Whittey, though he didn't sound pleased about it. "Ask not for whom the bell tolls..."

"Senhor?" Was the man insane after all? Was that his way out?

The carriage halted, and with a jolt, Almeida realized they were at the gates of the Envoy's building. His gaze flew back to Whittey.

Mrs. Whittey reached across and picked up the document case while Almeida's heart drummed with fear. She opened the case, took out the bag of coins and tossed the case back on the seat beside him.

"Goodbye, senhor," Whittey said. "For now."

He alighted from the carriage and handed down his wife before closing the door. He even had the nerve to issue further orders to Almeida's coachman, but at least as the couple sauntered through the gates and toward the Envoy's office, they did so alone. And his carriage took him home.

"HE WAS ACTING ALONE," Piers told Jeffery, when, after being shown into the private office with April, he once again faced the diplomat over his cherry wood desk. "And from motives of sheer greed. He has less idea than I do where Major Withan is."

"I confess I'm shocked," Jeffery said. He looked it. "So much for nobility! The lazy devil even slept soundly all night before deigning to turn up to collect his filthy lucre. Where is he now?"

Piers shrugged. "At his house, I assume, or his office if he has one."

"You let him go?" There was disapproval as well as surprise in Jeffery's voice.

"He is no use to me," Piers said. "Have him arrested if you like. I thought Sir Charles might prefer not to begin a diplomatic row, but that is his affair. I still have to find Withan."

Jeffery's gaze turned curious. "This Lord Petteril must care for his cousin a great deal to have wished you upon us. And yet, while Withan was glad enough to boast of the connection, he did not give me the impression that they were close."

"They are not," Piers agreed. Suddenly tired, it was an effort even to quirk his lips upwards. "His lordship appears to have an unexpectedly strong sense of family. I'm sure it surprises him as much as you."

"You know him?" Jeffery asked, curiosity standing out in his eyes.

"We've met," Piers said. He rose from his seat and held April's chair, seeing how close she was to falling asleep. "You will excuse us. I must take my wife back to the hotel."

"Of course." It was clearly on the tip of his tongue to ask if she had actually been with Whittey while he waited for the ransom to be collected, but he bit it back. Instead, rising with them, he asked, "What will you do now?"

"No idea," Piers said vaguely. "I daresay something will occur to me. Good morning."

Outside, she took his arm without him offering. It was her form of comfort, and she didn't touch easily.

"You must be shattered," he said.

"No. My brain's too busy. I need my notebook and peace to study it. We need to go back to the beginning, review everything."

"You don't want to sleep?" he asked in surprise.

"I slept in the church." Remembering, she blushed.

He pretended not to see. It was another moment to cherish, to take out and glance at occasionally before locking it back up. "Then let's go and wash and change and be comfortable again. And then we can decide what to do next."

DESPITE THEIR CONVERSATION, when he emerged from his dressing room some time later, refreshed and smart in formal morning dress, he half-expected to find her asleep on the bed or on the sofa.

Instead, she was seated on the balcony, poring over her notebook.

"Someone we have already talked to has the key to this," she said.

"Possibly. Even if it's only that he left Lisbon and fell into the wrong hands en route to Cuidad Rodrigo." He leaned on the stone balustrade, frowning down at the bustling street.

"Do you believe that?" she asked.

"It was always a possibility. His trunk is gone. I just couldn't believe he would be reckless enough to set out on such a journey without protection. Why didn't this other officer wait for him?"

"And did something really happen between him and the late Conde de Cartaxo the night before?"

He straightened. "More questions to be asked. But first, breakfast. Shall we, Mrs. Whittey?"

"Oh, yes!" She sprang up, shoving book and pencil into her reticule. "I'm so hungry I could almost eat that tentacly thing you were shovelling in yesterday."

"Octopus," Piers said severely. "And I never shovel my food."

"Ha."

"Although it was very good..."

At their favourite bakery, they consumed lots of coffee, bread and pastries—no octopus—and discussed their next port of call.

"The condessa," Piers decided. "There are far too many unanswered questions surrounding her and her late husband."

April nodded. "And then Captain Everett? Or someone else who can tell us about the officer who didn't wait for the major."

Piers nodded and took a handful of coins from his pocket to leave on the table.

Chapter Nine

Over the same garden gate through which they had seen Almeida leave the condessa's garden yesterday, April spotted a gardener at work.

"It might be our only chance to speak to her servants," she said, slowing her walk. "I'll go and ask him silly questions about those pink flowers. I've never seen them in England." Not, to be fair, that she had seen that many flowers in England at all, but she had *begun* to enjoy them.

"Good idea," his lordship said, lounging under the shade of a sycamore tree. "I'll watch for anyone looking worried."

April was already through the gate and sauntering up the path. She paused to admire the riot of bright pink flowers, even crouched down and removed her glove to feel the soil. She was aware of the gardener straightening from his weeding and watching her. And of the array of windows in the house, opened to the air before the sun moved around. Most houses inspired her with a sense of atmosphere. From this one, she got little. A house of secrets?

As though she had just noticed him, April smiled at the gardener and walked directly up to him. He bowed, jerkily, his dark, heavily lined face wary.

"*Bom dia*," she said cheerfully. "My husband and I are just about to call on the condessa and I could not help admiring this beautiful garden! Tell me, what is this gorgeous flower called, and what kind of conditions does it like? Would it thrive in England?"

The gardener snatched off his hat and bowed again, looking utterly baffled.

"Sorry," April confided. "I'm English. I don't have any Portuguese. I was just asking about those flowers and how I would look after them in England?" This time, she touched the petals and mimed planting and watering, then pointed at the increasingly hot sun.

The man made a helpless gesture, spreading his hands apologetically. "*Desculpe-me, senhora*." He pointed to the house, then back at his work and shambled off.

April returned to Lord Petteril who straightened under his tree and gave her his arm once more. "No luck?" he concluded.

"Not much. But he *is* afraid."

Petteril blinked, but he didn't ask her how she knew. She recognized fear in most forms. "Of what?" he wondered.

"Or who?" April murmured. She frowned. "Of *whom*?" After a moment, just before they went in by the front gate, she added. "He never smiled. Not once."

Neither did the other servants, although they were admitted at once and this time were shown straight into the same pretty room at the back of the house. Glancing at the lace covered window, through which a gentle flower-scented breeze flowed, April could not see the gardener or the place she had accosted him.

"My early birds," the condessa greeted them, rising from her chair with the barest hint of mockery. "What might I do for you today?"

They sat on the sofa she indicated, and she resumed her previous chair.

"When last we met," Lord Petteril said apologetically, "you said you would like to know the progress of my investigation. I am afraid to say it has not progressed at all."

"I am sorry to hear that," the condessa said as the manservant wheeled in a trolley laden with the same tea service they had seen before. "Though not entirely surprised." She waved the servant away and proceeded to pour the tea herself. The servant left. He didn't smile either, but nor did he look afraid. Perhaps the gardener was just a fearful kind of man.

Lord Petteril rose to ferry the cups destined for himself and April, a courtesy which still seemed very odd to her.

"I always doubted that there was much to learn here in Lisbon," the condessa continued. "All the questions have been asked."

"Then you believe Major Withan left the city?"

The condessa smiled sadly. "Certainly, he does not appear to be in it. Have you had a wasted journey, Mr. Whittey? Or will you pursue the matter into Spain?"

"I shall pursue the matter," Petteril said vaguely, taking a sip of tea. "I am no closer to Major Within than I was the last time we spoke, but I have learned some important things about the people who surrounded him during his short stay."

"Such as?" the condessa prompted, although she did not look terribly interested in the answer.

"Such as the poverty of certain nobles. I had not realized how hard the war has hit, financially speaking. It cannot be easy for the rich to be suddenly poor."

"I don't suppose it is ever easy to be poor," the condessa countered. "It is not a condition, fortunately, that has ever assailed me."

"Then your husband left you well provided for? I am glad."

"Do you take an interest in your late husband's business?" April asked.

"Of course. I always did."

April smiled as dazzlingly as she knew how. "Good for you, senhora. In England, married ladies are expected to merely ornament drawing rooms and dinner parties."

"I expect it was you," Petteril said, "who advised him to diversify from merely arms to medicines."

After the bland admiration, this clearly took the condessa by surprise. Her cup paused in mid air and her eyes narrowed. But only for an instant. She sipped her tea. "You have indeed been busy—er...learning. Soldiers need medical supplies."

"I believe Senhor de Almeida lacked your foresight and is now struggling in many ways."

The condessa set down her cup in its saucer. "With respect, Mr. Whittey, I fail to see how such *learning* brings you closer to Major Withan."

Petteril smiled apologetically. "Being short of funds makes one vulnerable," he said vaguely. "To manipulation, temptation... One can make wrong decisions."

"Are you asking me if Senhor de Almeida made any? As I am sure you know, he and my husband did not agree on many issues. We are not friends."

"Condessa," Petteril said, reprovingly, "You are much more than friends. He longs to elope with you."

For the first time, the condessa's control slipped. Her tea slopped over the edge of the cup into the saucer, and she set them both down on the table beside her. By then, she had herself better in hand.

"He is a foolish man in many ways," she said, with a shade of affectionate contempt that was more damning than any downright insult would have been. "A little excitement, a little pleasure to pass the time is not the grand affair. He has an expensive wife and a failing business. He does not need love, he needs money. His only hope is to marry off that insipid daughter, only no one will take her off his hands."

Interesting, thought April. Her only spiteful insult was against Eliana. Was that significant?

Presumably his lordship wondered the same thing, for he said, "Senhorita de Almeida does not believe Major Withan is dead."

"With respect to the senhorita," drawled the condessa, "what does she know? She can hardly have spoken to him. Although he was just the kind of handsome, charming man whose polite attentions would mislead a plain young girl."

"Grounds for a duel," Lord Petteril said lightly, "only with Almeida, not your late husband."

The condessa sighed with exaggerated patience. "Mr. Whittey, I am in no need of protection. My husband died outside a bordello. The false myth of a duel is quite unnecessary."

"But he didn't," Petteril said.

The condessa blinked. "I beg your pardon?"

"The conde did not die outside the bordello. At least not outside the one where he was found. His body was moved there after his death."

Now he had all the condessa's attention. "How can you possibly know that?"

"There was no blood in the road."

Was that relief in the condessa's face? Perhaps, but she looked merely amused as she mocked, "And from that you deduce he fought a duel with Major Withan?"

"Do you know that he didn't?" April asked.

The condessa glanced at her in surprise, as though she had forgotten her presence. She was probably the kind of woman who ignored her own sex. "No, I don't. I only know my husband."

"Who did not like Britain or the British alliance," Petteril pointed out. "Do you?"

"I am a realist, sir. I deal with the world as it is, not as I would like it to be. And my husband was too great a man to fight duels over trivial political disagreements. Do you imagine he and Major Withan killed each other? Then who buried the major? I wish you better fortune in your enquiries, Mr. Whittey, but truly, you will not find the answer in my late husband!"

"SHE IS PROBABLY RIGHT," Lord Petteril said as they left the condessa's house. "Although I would like to know why a wife would rather believe her husband died at a brothel instead of in a duel of honour."

"Perhaps she doesn't care how he died," April speculated. "Perhaps she prefers the dishonour so she doesn't have to feel guilty about her liaison with Almeida."

"Do you think she feels guilty?" Petteril wondered. "Shall we walk back and speak to Everett?"

In fact, Captain Everett hailed them from a streetside eating house near his lodgings. "Come and join me," he said. "I do hate eating alone. Soon I won't have to—the quacks say I can ride again and rejoin my regiment next week."

"Good news," Petteril said, watching as the captain held April's chair for her. "Your leg seems all the stronger for our mad dash to the cart the other day."

Everett grinned. "It didn't seem so at the time, but next day I walked further than before and it's getting better all the time. How are you getting on? Found out any more about poor Withan?"

"Nothing that makes much sense. We thought for a little we had a kidnap and ransom, but it turned out to be a hum. There are unanswered questions in Lisbon, but I'm looking seriously at the possibility that he really did leave the city."

"Pretty sure he did," Everett said, signalling the woman inside to bring more food for his friends.

"Tell me about this Captain Hood," Petteril said. "The officer he was supposed to travel with."

Everett, who had been smiling at April just a little too long, blinked and blushed. "Decent fellow. Good officer."

"Then why did he not wait for Withan?"

Everett shrugged. "Thought he would catch up."

"Why? Hood travelled ahead with other soldiers, knowing the country. How could Withan, new to Portugal and Spain and, frankly, to war, catch up safely with experienced soldiers?"

Everett shifted uncomfortably. "Put like that it sounds negligent, if not positively spiteful. Not a spiteful fellow, Hood."

"How well did they know each other in Lisbon?" April asked, wondering if she should have just one slice of bread. It was rather delicious dipped in olive oil instead of slathered with butter... "Were they acquainted before that?"

"Not before, I don't think. But they got on well enough here."

"Well enough," Lord Petteril pounced. "Then they were not friends?"

Everett looked flustered. "Withan was only here a week. Hardly enough time to become blood brothers."

"True," Petteril agreed. "And Withan could be such a cocky creature."

"He could," Everett said gratefully. "Raised a few hackles with men of battlefield experience."

"Not surprised. Did he annoy you?"

Everett closed his mouth, a look of alarm entering his face. "Yes, if you must know. A little. But I knew he'd learn."

"And Hood?"

"Oh, he irritated Hood, but that was less to do with war than with women."

April sat up. "Hood went to the brothel with the major."

Everett's face flamed a fiery red.

"You *all* went," she said.

"Not the night before he left," Everett muttered. "We went once when we were drunk, shortly after Withan arrived. Hood and Withan fell out over a girl. Hardly a quarrel worth pursuing. The girl was bought by the higher bidder."

"And yet Hood bore a grudge," Petteril speculated. "Did you?"

"If you must know I didn't join in the dashed auction. Got my eye on a different kind of lady entirely. Though I daresay Withan ousted me there, too."

"Eliana de Almeida," April said. It was an instinctive guess, blurted aloud to see Everett's reaction. And it certainly got one.

Everett paled. "How the devil did you know that?"

"I didn't," April said apologetically. "We just knew she liked Major Withan."

"I'm a nobody," Everett said fiercely. "A career officer. She would never be allowed to look at a man like me. Even if she wanted to. I never pursued her. Only met her once."

Petteril leaned forward. "How often did Hood meet her?"

"I don't know. He was already acquainted with her family, somehow, before I came here last month."

"And then Withan stepped in..." Petteril mused. "Do you think it annoyed Captain Hood so much that when Withan was late meeting them, he just went on without him?"

"I'm sure he looked out for signs of him the whole way," Everett muttered.

He was a good man, loyal to a fault, April reflected. Like a schoolboy lying to protect a friend from punishment.

Petteril nodded and was silent for a little as they tucked into some sardines and toasted bread.

"And so you rejoin your regiment next week?" Petteril said, as though changing the subject.

"I do."

Petteril picked up his wine glass. "May I tag along with you?"

FORTUNATA DE ALMEIDA had known the moment her husband came home. She waited several hours but he did not join her, even though he should not have been at the house. He should have been at his government office.

Which meant he was ashamed of something.

Damn Beatriz de Cartaxo. Of course, the true betrayal was Duarte's. Beatriz would have cast him aside long before now if he hadn't kept going back. And perhaps if Fortunata had not made her own interest in Major Withan quite so obvious.

The major had upset the balance of their marriage. Fortunata had never been short of admirers. She had merely been too well-bred to do anything about them. Until Withan. It had been unusually sweet to bask in the admiration of such a handsome and aristocratic a man. No wonder Duarte had noticed...

She realized she was staring into space and blinked. It was time, she thought irreverently, for the mountain to go to Mohammed. Accordingly, she rose and glided along the passage to Duarte's study. She did not knock.

Duarte sat slumped behind his huge, ornate desk, on which resided no papers of state or even books to be consulted. She had the impression he had been sitting there for hours without moving. He did not even rise when he eventually saw her come toward him.

She sat down in the chair on the other side of the desk. "What have you done?"

He stirred but did not even think of lying. "I was stupid. I thought I had found a way to revive our fortunes. I wrote a ransom note for the British major and collected the money. It would have solved our most immediate troubles, given us a fresh start."

Given *you* a fresh start, Fortunata thought with a spurt of anger. *With Beatriz, only she won't go, will she? So you are reduced to me once more, and you don't even know you are better off.*

"I have some ideas of my own about solving those troubles," she said. "To begin—"

"It is worse than that," Duarte interrupted. "The ransom money was laid as a trap by the Englishman Whittey. I am found out. And he took back what coin there was. Even that, a mere quarter of what I asked, would have helped."

"Have you told Beatriz that?" she asked steadily.

He didn't even look surprised that she knew, only wriggled with a hint of impatience. "Of course not. She knows nothing about it. It was my own idea and it almost worked. But now, thanks to the Englishman, I have nothing. My career is no doubt ruined. I could be arrested. I cannot even keep my wife and daughter, let alone come up with dowry enough for anyone to marry Eliana."

"There is a little money kept aside for Eliana," she reminded him. "She is of the ancient nobility and her father is a trusted member of the Regent's government. Whittey will have neither the wish nor the influence to ruin you."

"Sir Charles might."

"Sir Charles is a pragmatist. As for the dowry, we must use it immediately to good effect."

"There will be rumours," Duarte said wearily. "That is inevitable. Eliana is not beautiful enough or charming enough to win a husband despite so modest a dowry. What chance does she have when the rumours begin?"

"The rumours are unlikely to reach England."

He blinked, focusing on her face at last. "England? What does England have to do with it?"

"Everything," Fortunata replied. "Major Withan was English. His cousin, Lord Petteril is English and far away. You will write a letter to the lord, both condoling the loss of his cousin and explaining how his pursuit has ruined Eliana's reputation. His death has left her alone and unmarriageable. A good man will make reparation for his kinsman's crimes. We are prepared to offer him our well-born daughter, if his settlements are good enough."

"He'll run a mile!" Duarte exclaimed. "Even if he is not married already."

"He is not, and he won't. According to the major, he is of a quixotic nature and will always do what he perceives to be the right thing. I'm sure he knows his cousin the major well enough to believe an intended seduction of our daughter at the very least."

Duarte sat up. "You really think it will work?" he said eagerly.

"I do."

"It would solve many, many problems!"

More than you know.

Chapter Ten

As they walked back to the hotel, Piers said, "Do you believe that? That they all love Eliana de Almeida?"

"You think she is not beautiful enough to inspire devotion?"

Piers considered. "In such numbers, frankly, yes. She is quick, intelligent, loyal, and determined. I rather like her myself, but we are talking about Bertie who I doubt has ever loved anyone except the man in the looking glass, and who has never had a mistress who was not a diamond of *some* water or other." He looked thoughtful. "Although I wouldn't put it past him to pay court to Eliana just to wind up the others."

April was silent for a few steps. "What I understood from Everett's revelations was that neither of them looked at Eliana until the major did. Do you not notice how her face changes when she speaks of him?"

Piers opened his mouth to disparage just folly, only when he thought back to the reception and to the breakfast with Eliana, he suddenly saw her point. He hadn't really noticed because he was not looking at her like that for any number of reasons. He doubted he would recognize the girl if she stood in front of him, but he did remember the sudden radiance of her eyes, and the charm of a smiling expression.

"Then Bertie's quarrel with Hood at the bordello was not really about a whore, but about Eliana... And that might well be reason enough for Hood to have deliberately left Bertie to his fate. Damn Bertie, he is his own worst enemy."

There was another point, of course. If Bertie had become genuinely attached to Eliana, why would he have gone to the brothel at all? The first drunken visit could be excused since he probably had not yet met

Eliana. But he had gone back the night before he left Lisbon, and then gone on to say a fond and possibly passionate farewell to Eliana. Anathema to Piers, but perhaps not to his more hedonistic cousin.

Still, it niggled at him.

"Are we really going with Captain Everett next week?" April asked innocently.

He glanced at her somewhat dubiously. He cared neither to leave her behind unprotected in the city, nor to take her into the kind of danger that seemed to have done for Bertie. Well, he had several days to consider that conundrum, and he had no intention of fighting before it was necessary.

"I'm considering it," he said blandly.

He was considering a very different visit, too, and he really, really couldn't have April with him on that one.

AT THE HOTEL, DEEP in thought, Piers sat on a chair, idly twirling his walking stick between his fingers. April, on the sofa, was scribbling furiously into her notebook. Reading and writing lessons had been suspended for the trip, but it was time her education advanced.

At home, she chose all kinds of books to read, from novels to travel and history, and once he had caught her wrestling with the plays of Shakespeare. The teacher in him knew her studies should be more structured—perhaps he would direct it better when they returned home. And yet it was a pleasure to watch her devour whatever seized her avid if erratic attention, enjoying all the new worlds opened to her through the basic ability to read. She was like him in that.

And his mind had wandered from the point.

Using the stick as leverage, he rose to his feet and strolled to the door, picking up his hat on the way.

"I'm going out for five minutes. Wait here."

She glanced up. He knew she did because he felt her gaze on the back of his head. He closed the door quietly and ran downstairs.

Striding into the heat of the afternoon, he saw someone he thought was Dado, waiting hopefully in the shade for someone to guide. But he only raised one hand in greeting and hurried in the opposite direction.

Having no wish to exhaust himself rushing about in the blazing sun, he poked awake the snoozing driver of a hired carriage and directed it to the district from where, when Dado had taken them, they had walked to the brothel.

Again, it was the stench that assailed his senses first. Asking the driver to wait in the same shady spot, he made his way into the hot, narrow streets, winding upward and around corners. His eyes watered. How could people live in this? Like anything else, he supposed one got used to it.

The deeper he delved, the more the buildings on either side seemed to close in on him. It was similar to St. Giles's back streets in many ways, and as he picked his way through the filth, he kept his eyes watchful and his posture confident. Most of all, he kept moving. Dark eyes glittering with malevolence watched him from cracks in the walls. A couple of youths on what had once been a doorstep looked him up and down and apparently decided against any move. He darted forward in the nick of time to avoid a deluge of waste landing on him from a window above and strode on with perfect aplomb. His shudders were inward.

After a couple of false turns, he found the street of the bordello. Not for the first time, he wondered why he should find it so easy to recognize buildings, while faces might as well have no features at all for all they stayed in his wayward mind.

Worse, he had got lazy, relying on April so much since they had arrived here. But this was no time to allow anxiety.

In the quiet, empty street, he rapped sharply on the brothel door.

It was opened faster than he expected by a very large man. Piers had no idea if they had met before.

"Divina, *por favor*," he said briefly, taking the large man by surprise when he brushed past him into the house, which smelled almost as rank as the street.

The large man held out a meaty palm in the gloom. Piers dropped a few coins into it. The man's fingers twitched commandingly. Piers stared at him.

"Divina," he repeated.

Apparently deciding he could not be intimidated at this stage, the man broke eye contact and led him along the passage to the end.

"Divina!" he yelled and pushed open the door without further warning.

Piers tightened his grip on his sword stick, half-expecting attack from behind as well as in front. But the room before him was empty of all save a dark young woman in a half-open robe.

He gazed at her intently. *Was* this the same girl he had spoken to before? All the Portuguese seemed to have dark hair and eyes so there was no help there. The girl called Divina, whom he presumed had been Bertie's favourite, had a torn ear, he recalled, as though an earring had been ripped from it at one time. This girl's mass of curly hair was hiding her ears.

He reached up to push back her hair and a beefy hand clamped over his wrist. The girl jerked back out of the way, but in the movement, he glimpsed her damaged ear. He smiled and with his free hand, held out a coin to her.

The large man grunted, released him, and walked out, pulling the door closed behind him.

The girl dropped her coin into a box and wrapped both arms around Piers's neck.

"Tell me," he said, "about Major Withan."

Her arms went slack but did not release him. "Major Bertie? You like men?"

Reaching up, Piers detached her arms from his neck and led her to sit on the rumpled, none too clean bed.

Taking another coin from his pocket, he said, "Did he come to you?"

The girl's eyes fixed on the coin. "Once. Vigorous man."

"I'm sure. Did he come alone or with companions?"

"They have one each." She smirked. "All choose me. I choose Major Bertie."

"Did they quarrel?"

Scorn entered her eyes. "Over a whore? They were not so drunk. Why we talk about other men? Tauro come and throw you out soon."

He caught her questing hand, pressing the coin into it. "The night before the Conde de Cartaxo was found dead in the street, did he come here?"

She shrugged. "I don't see him. He come once, months ago. I don't think he like whores."

"But your Major Bertie, he came here that night."

"He ask for me, Divina," she said proudly.

"What did he say to you?"

She blinked. "Say? I am whore, not his mother."

"Divina."

She stared at him. "You are like him." Without releasing the coin, she touched his face with something approaching wonder, running her fingers across his cheekbone and down to his chin. "Is he your brother?"

"Cousin," Piers said.

Her hand fell to her lap. "He come to say goodbye. Next day he go to the army. He give me the present."

"What did he give you?" Not the flowers. He had not bought those then.

She opened her hand to reveal the coin Piers had given her. "Some of this." She raised her eyes to Piers's. "Then he go. He not touch me. This is respect. He like me."

"He must have," Piers said gravely. "He didn't pay you the first time, did he?"

There was mischief in the girl's smile. "I cover for him. Lope never knows. Major Bertie pays me back. He is a good man."

Not many people called Bertie a good man. But he had no need to come here, to even remember the girl he had used and yet he had paid his dues, made things right before embarking on his new life.

There had been a growing self-disgust in Bertie. It had been there when he had asked Piers to buy him his transfer to the Peninsula. It seemed April could be right about Eliana too. She could be part of the same growth.

"Yes, perhaps he is," Piers said. "How long did he stay with you?"

She wrinkled her nose. "Not five minutes."

"And he didn't fight with anyone?"

She shook her head. "He see only me and Lope."

"Did he say where he was going next?"

She sighed. "No, but I think to a lady."

Petteril stood up and felt in his pocket. Leaving enough to pay the driver waiting for him, he took out the rest of his coins and gave them to her.

"Hide them. Save them and get out. This life is too short."

Her lips parted. Her eyes widened.

On sudden impulse, he said, "Divina, who owns this place? Who owns the building?"

She laughed. "Conde de Cartaxo. That was the joke."

His mind spinning, Piers walked out of the room—and straight into a thin, malnourished man with malevolent black eyes.

"You again," he hissed.

Lope the brothel keeper. Piers knew him because he appeared to be wearing the same clothes.

"And indeed, you again," Piers murmured, twirling his stick, although in such a confined space, it was next to useless. Lope could do much more damage with a knife. If he chose. "I paid," he said casually. "Ask the giant. And the girl."

"Don't come back," Lope said as Piers sauntered past, skin prickling.

"I won't," Piers assured him. He paused before the front door.

The large man lurked on the stairs behind him. Lope had followed Piers along the passage.

"I won't find your bravos awaiting me in the street, will I?" Piers asked.

Lope smiled evilly. "Not my bravos. Men who ask so many questions make a lot of enemies."

Well, I can't stay here forever... He opened the front door, his heart hammering, and walked out into the empty street. But there was little sense of relief. Even in the bright sunshine, threat seemed to lurk all around him, behind every sullen face and every half-opened door, every window, every alley. It took all his effort to maintain the confident demeanour of the dangerous clerk which he had invented back in March to search for April. How naïve he had been then...

And yet in some bizarre way, he was actually enjoying himself. Mixed with all those warning prickles, was a shiver of excitement because he was approaching a solution. It was in his grasp, if only he could put it together...

He found the driver of his hired carriage asleep and poked him for the second time with his walking stick, before climbing into the carriage and mulling over what he had learned.

APRIL DID NOT ACTUALLY mind when Lord Petteril went out without her. For one thing, she had always understood his need for solitude and they had been living in each other's pockets for a fortnight. At least on the ship, he could lose himself on the deck. Or she could. Here in the hotel, he had to shut himself in the poky little dressing room or go out alone.

April, to whom companionship was still novel and rather wonderful, did not feel cramped, except in that she could not easily do what his lordship disapproved of. She might be pretending but she was *not* his wife or his equal. She was his employee, his assistant, and she was supposed to obey.

On the other hand...

When the door closed behind him, she set aside her notebook and pencil and went on to the balcony. She saw him emerge from the front of the hotel, clap his hat on his head and raise a hand to Dado before striding off down the street.

She had hoped he was going to talk to Dado. Since he wasn't, she went back into the room, put on her wide-brimmed straw hat and left, locking the door behind her and dropping the key into her reticule.

Dado was trying to persuade a red-faced English merchant and his equally flushed wife that they wanted to tour the city while it was quiet. When they had brushed him off with impatience, April walked up to him.

"Can we talk, Dado?"

He whisked off his hat. "Senhora, of course!" He smiled. "I was afraid you take me in dislike."

"Not dislike," she assured him. "Perhaps distrust, a little. Because of the men who found us at the bordello."

He did not look surprised. In fact, a haughty look entered his face, almost worthy of Lord Petteril's aunt. "Those men are nothing to do with me."

"No, but they knew where to find us and not many people were aware where we were going. If it makes you feel better, we don't entirely trust Captain Everett either."

"Captain Everett is a good man with too little to do. He needs to be back with the army. But he has no reason and less ability to send *bandidos* against your husband. Or anyone else."

That he defended Everett convinced April that she was right about him. But then, she was always more inclined to instinct than evidence. For Lord Petteril's sake, she said, "But you do know the brothel keeper, Lope. You said what he wanted you to."

Dado shrugged. "No one but a fool crosses Lope. I said nothing to mislead your husband."

"Then the conde never went to the bordello?"

"I saw him enter once, perhaps in January or February. I took some officers there—Lope pays me for that. But I never see him there before or since. Why would I? He has—had —a beautiful wife."

No one ever says a man has a clever wife, April reflected. As if all a woman ever had in her favour was her looks. And her husband. Even when she seemed to be the one with the genius for business.

"I don't suppose," she said apologetically, "that you ever saw Duarte de Almeida there?"

"I don't know him."

"It strikes me," April mused, "that he would be more likely to fight a duel with Cartaxo than Major Withan would." Only why move his body? "What of Captain Hood? Do you know him?"

"He spends his leave here. I show him the city."

"Is he the sort of man to take offence?"

Dado's eyes were direct. "Do you mean, would he leave Major Withan to travel alone, just from spite?"

"It crossed my mind," April admitted. "It seems to have crossed yours too."

Dado hesitated. She could almost see him running through the different answers he could give to make her more comfortable, or more friendly toward him, or more grateful. His gaze re-focused on her. He was no older than she. For a moment, she was Ape again, wary survivor of the streets, just like Dado.

Perhaps he recognized it in her face, for his eyes widened. "The officers on leave, they banter, they quarrel, they even fall out. But they look after each other."

April nodded slowly. "But Major Withan was new. He didn't have that brotherhood."

Dado thought. "Withan's rank is higher. Hood might give him a fright, but he would not abandon him. As for Withan, he was no fool."

"Was," April repeated bleakly. "Everyone keeps saying *was*." And yet, was the likeliest scenario not that Hood had been teaching his green superior a lesson that had gone tragically wrong?

Dado was looking beyond her to people emerging from the hotel, so she left him to it and returned to the room to make some more notes. It seemed likely they would be making a trip into Spain, perhaps as far as the stronghold of Cuidad Rodrigo. With nostalgia, she wondered if Lord Petteril would allow her to travel in male clothes. He might consider she was safer that way.

She caught sight of herself in the looking glass, sitting on the sofa in her blue muslin gown, hair up, pencil in hand, and blinked. She laughed. Who would have thought she could look anything like that? Even more surprisingly, she rather liked it.

Chapter Eleven

April sat on the balcony, waiting with the first stirrings of anxiety for Lord Petteril to return.

It was odd to think that only a few months ago she had no idea who he was and yet now he had become the focus of her life. She didn't like not to know where he was. Apart from anything else, she could never rid herself of the knowledge that in towns at least, he needed her to look after him. He had come a long way, certainly, learned loads for a nob, but he wasn't quite up to snuff.

She was also uneasily aware that if he found his cousin's body, or other proof of his death, he would suffer. She didn't let herself remember too often how he had been the night she had first met him, so lost and alone and swaying towards the edge of the high balcony...

It terrified her.

Below, in the empty street, a carriage rumbled into view and disgorged the long, lean figure of Lord Petteril.

Delighted, she jumped to her feet and leaned over the rail. Striding across the road to the hotel, he glanced up at the balcony, saw her waving, and smiled in the way that melted her silly heart. Mostly because she still wasn't used to people being pleased to see her. She was more used to kicks and blows. She had never imagined having a friend like this.

Of course, this wasn't how it could be back home. She wouldn't be dancing across the room to open her bedchamber door for him!

She did now, however, all but dragging him into the room. "Where have you been?" she demanded sternly, and then, without waiting for a reply, "I've been talking to Dado, and those ruffians at the bordello did *not* come from him, which means either the condessa or your friends at the embassy."

"Or Almeida, who, as we know, keeps company with the condessa. I don't think they're important."

Deflated, she took his hat from him and threw it on to the side table where it landed perfectly.

"On the other hand," he added, "it's good to know we can trust him. We might yet need him before this is done. And Everett." He took off his coat and tugged at his cravat to loosen it before sinking down on the sofa. "I went back to the bordello."

Oh dear God. She sank into a crouch at his feet. "Alone?"

"Didn't want to appear threatening," he said apologetically. "Guess who owns the building?"

"Lope?"

"The Conde de Cartaxo. So it will be the Condessa's, now."

She sat back on her heels. "What does that mean?" she asked slowly.

"I'm not sure, but it means something. It all means something, but this heat makes it hard to think."

She rose and went to the jug of lemonade she had ordered earlier and poured him a glass, thrusting it into his hand. He smiled at her in gratitude, but she was still far too rattled to forgive him yet.

"I'm meant to tell you when I go somewhere dangerous," she said, scowling. "You should have told me."

"I couldn't. You'd have found a way to follow me."

"Good thing if I had! You need me to watch your back."

"In many ways that would have been a lot more comfortable," he admitted. "But I still couldn't do it. Anyway, I got in and out alive and I'm beginning to think you might be right about Bertie and Eliana de Almeida. His last night in Lisbon that we know of, he went to pay back the girl Divina for her earlier services. He didn't stay with her. He was merely settling his affairs before he left the city."

"More than he did before he left London," April muttered. "Suppose he didn't have you in Lisbon."

"It's clearly good for him. Also, Divina says the officers never quarrelled over her but over some lady who preferred Bertie."

"Eliana." April sat down beside Petteril. "Could this all be about Eliana? Did her father discover her liking for Bertie and, needing a richer husband for her, get rid of him?"

"Almeida could have *made* Bertie late to meet Captain Hood in the morning," Petteril murmured, "and crossed his fingers something would happen."

"Or paid some ruffians to go after him."

Petteril met her gaze. "I'm not sure it looks good for Bertie."

"Or for Almeida," April said grimly. "Innocent of holding the major for ransom, but not necessarily of murder."

They both contemplated that for a little. Lord Petteril had a deep frown between his brows.

"The trouble is," he said at last, "I don't think Almeida is nearly as clever as he thinks he is. Either in Lisbon or on the road to Cuidad Rodrigo, could he really have committed murder so carefully, and hidden the body so well that no one ever found it?"

"Possibly not," April said. "But maybe the senhora could."

Petteril inclined his head. "Maybe. But is *she* so clever? She believed Bertie was in love with her when everyone else knew he was pursuing Eliana—with what intention is open to interpretation. Also, I don't like coincidences. Is it not odd if both Bertie and Cartaxo died the same night?"

"Two nobs," April said thoughtfully. "Yes, that's unusual. But if they go to places like that bordello, they take their chances."

"Why would Lope murder his landlord? It's not as if he would inherit the building. Why would he murder a lucrative client? Although to be sure Bertie wasn't so lucrative if he didn't pay." He sighed and rubbed his forehead. "None of this makes any sense, and yet I keep feeling we're on the cusp of understanding and then it all slides away again."

"You got no sleep last night," she said gruffly. "It will make more sense tomorrow. I think we need to talk to Eliana again before we go haring off with Captain Everett."

If he noticed her inclusion in the expedition, he gave no sign of it. "We'll go tomorrow," he agreed. "Speak to all the Almeidas, in fact."

THEY BREAKFASTED EARLY the following morning, after retiring early. Piers felt somewhat sharper, but either some of the pieces were still missing from the puzzle of Bertie's disappearance, or he was still incapable of putting them in the right order.

April's sunny commentary on the passers-by and Lisbon life was cheering and welcome. In fact, he felt a strong tug of longing just to keep sitting where he was, watching the world go by and drinking coffee in the sunshine, exchanging occasional, amusing chatter with the only person in the world who never judged him.

Was that self-pity? he wondered, revolted, and promptly rose to his feet, though it was too early to call on the Almeidas.

"Let's go and plan our campaign," he said, since he found it impossible to sit down again.

April rose willingly enough, and they strolled around the corner to the hotel.

She said, "There's that Kelvin going into the hotel. With Mr. Jeffery."

"Really?"

As one, they sped up and encountered both men in the foyer. Even for Piers, they were easy enough to tell apart.

"Has something happened?" he asked quickly. "Not another ransom demand?"

"No, we don't *think* so," Jeffery said. "Is there somewhere private we can talk?"

"Come up," April invited.

On some level, behind the anxiety, it both amused and impressed him how well April had taken to the role of easy-going yet welcoming hostess. She was highly observant, of course, but he thought some of it was her own nature, a glimpse of how she could have been born into a different environment. How she could still be, with a good, hard-working young husband and a home of her own.

He wanted those things for her, even if he ached at the same time. Of course, she didn't want them for herself, or not yet...

As before, when Kelvin had called on them, Piers rested against the arm of April's chair. Jeffery took a sealed packet from inside his coat and held it in front of him like a trophy. Or a weapon.

"This was delivered to the office this morning," he said, "with a covering letter to Sir Charles, asking him to forward it by diplomatic channels to Lord Petteril."

Piers blinked. "Petteril? Who is it from?"

"Duarte de Almeida," said Kelvin, glaring at him.

"How curious," Piers murmured. "Why would Almeida write to Petteril?"

"That's what we wondered," Jeffery said. "In truth, we should not have removed this from the building, but it seemed quicker than summoning you. I felt it might be pertinent to your investigation, considering Lord Petteril's relationship to Major Withan, and his lordship's influence behind your presence in Lisbon."

"I see," Piers said, refraining from snatching the letter.

"We disagreed," Jeffery added, "Kelvin and I, over whether Sir Charles should not be given the letter first. But Sir Charles would not open it. He would merely send it on and then we would not know if it was relevant to your enquiries."

"I only countenance this at all," Kelvin said fussily, "because of Senhor Almeida's unfortunate behaviour yesterday."

"So you must decide whether or not to open it," Jeffery finished. "After which, we are both here to see to its return to Sir Charles's desk."

"It is probably a mere letter of condolence," Kelvin said.

Piers reached out and took the letter from Jeffery's fingers. "Let us find out. I believe his lordship would expect me to read it."

He almost expected April to snort. She remained silent as he leaned back and broke the seal. Unfolding it, he read about half of it and was so astonished that he went back to the beginning to be sure he had understood the overly formal English.

It was he who snorted, and with quite inappropriate laughter. "It is a proposal of marriage, couched in terms of healing his lordship's grief and compensating the beautiful young lady in question for the broken promises—and questionable courtship—of Major Withan. Someone should tell Almeida that Petteril is not really rich enough to dig him out of his financial mess."

"Bare-faced impudence!" Jeffery exclaimed. "Does the man never tire of trying to rob his lordship blind?"

"Oh, I don't know," April said. "His lordship could do much worse than Eliana de Almeida."

"But could Eliana do worse than Lord Petteril?" Piers retorted.

"There, you have me."

Kelvin and Jeffery were glancing from one to the other, clearly baffled by the light-hearted exchange. Hastily, Piers returned to the letter, memorising its content before folding it and returning it to Jeffery.

"By all means, pass it on to Sir Charles for his lordship."

"You will make your own report to his lordship?" Jeffery said anxiously. "Before he might consider himself honour-bound in this matter?"

"Lord Petteril is more up to snuff than people think," April said unexpectedly.

"His lordship will be warmed by your approval," Piers said.

"So he should be."

"Then it does not really help with your investigation," Kelvin said, rising to his feet. "I knew we should not have brought it."

"On the contrary," Piers said. "It rather tells us that Almeida is desperate." Which was the perfect time to call upon his family.

ELIANA SAW THEM COMING. At least, Piers assumed it was Eliana. It was certainly not a maid. Her face bobbed briefly by one of the upper front windows, so he was not entirely surprised when she opened the front door before he had time to knock.

Seizing April's hand, she all but dragged them into the house and into a small reception room to the right.

"Thank God you are here," she exclaimed. "I wait and wait to hear from you. Sit. Tell me what you have learned."

That you would be better well away from the so-called care of your parents. "Nothing solid," he said aloud. "Except that no one is hidden at the addresses you gave us. However, your information has led us to several more ideas and we need to ask you a few more questions."

"Ask," she demanded, trying not to look too disappointed. April was right. Her face glowed when she spoke of Bertie, or in anticipation of hearing about him. Vitality—love, even—lent her beauty. He was not entirely surprised that after Bertie's arrival both Everett and Hood had looked on her in a different way.

"Before the major came to Lisbon," he asked, to be sure, "did you have a particular suitor? Or a favoured admirer?"

She shook her head. "Until the major, I prefer a convent." Her smile was not entirely happy. "The suitors prefer the convent option too."

"Nonsense," April said briskly. "We have met at least two young gentlemen who were most put out by your preference for the major."

Eliana's prominent dark eyebrows flew up. "Really? I can't imagine who."

"Then you do not know Captain Everett? Or Captain Hood?"

She frowned. "Captain Hood has a long leave, and was to take the major back with him. Everett has a broken leg."

"Did they come here to your parents' house?"

She thought. "I dance with Captain Hood at the Envoy's ball. He does his duty. They both call on my mother, once or twice when the major was with us, too."

She didn't describe them, thought of them only as to their connection with Bertie. Poor Eliana. Bertie was a shifting sand in which to anchor her hopes. Probably.

"Think," April urged. "Could you imagine either of them harming Major Withan?"

Eliana's eyes widened. "In what way?"

"Any way. A quarrel that went too far. A drunken fight. Playing a trick like leaving the city early and not waiting for him to catch up. Anything."

Her face whitened. "You think one of those things is what happened to him?"

"We have to be sure none of them did. And Captain Hood is not around to ask."

"I hardly know them," Eliana said desperately. "I cannot imagine them hurting one of their own, but how do I know? Major Withan was not always...conciliatory."

"Did he flaunt you?" April asked.

Eliana blinked. "He did not hide his interest."

"Then your parents knew?" Piers asked.

Eliana's lips twisted. "My parents are not observant. Major Withan is not wealthy enough or important enough to interest my father. And

Mama knows she is much more beautiful than me. She has no reason to see the major's interest."

And yet Eliana did not doubt it, transitory or otherwise.

"Then your parents never forbade you to see him again?" Piers asked.

"Why would they? He was about to leave Lisbon."

"Just supposing," April said, "one or both your parents had witnessed your secret farewell to Major Withan late that evening. What would they have done?"

"Told me he was unworthy and made sure he was never invited again, should he ever return to Lisbon."

"Your father would not have called him out?" Piers suggested. "Fought a duel with him?"

"Over *me*?" Eliana said in blatant disbelief.

Oh yes, it was time she left her parents' house.

"Speaking of my father," she added, with a glance at the window, "here he comes. I'm afraid he has seen us."

"No matter," Piers said. "I wish to speak to him too."

Almeida's face was pale, his hands visibly shaking when he strode into the room, but he held himself rigidly upright as he commanded Eliana to go to her mother.

Eliana glanced at April and Piers, hesitating as though she would somehow protect them, then bowed her head and obeyed.

"What are you doing in my home?" he demanded between stiff lips. "Turning my daughter against me now?"

"Oh, you seem to be making an excellent job of that on your own," Piers drawled, forgetting for a moment that he was not the viscount here.

Almeida's eyes narrowed. "What do you mean by that?"

"Think about it," Piers retorted. "Tell me, are you aware of a particular attachment between your daughter and any other man?"

Almeida flung back his head in outrage. "My daughter is pure!"

"Even the pure fall in love. Please answer the question."

"I see no reason why I should!" Almeida blustered.

"Don't you?" April said innocently, and yet Almeida blinked at her, all the false pride draining visibly from him.

"My daughter is not interested in men, which must be obvious to anyone in her company. More to the point, eligible men are not interest in her."

"Then you have no matrimonial hopes for her?" Piers asked innocently.

A faintly smug look flickered and vanished in Almeida's eyes. "I did not say that. My family is old and proud, and I have every faith that we will contract an advantageous alliance for her."

"Have you ever fought a duel, senhor?" April asked suddenly.

Baffled by the change of subject, he stared at her. "Not since I was a very silly young man."

"Then you did not fight with the Conde de Cartaxo?"

"No, nor anyone else in twenty years. Why should I?"

"For the honour of your daughter?" Piers suggested. "Or your wife?"

"No one would dare to impugn their honour," Almeida said haughtily. "They would have no cause and I find you offensive to suggest otherwise."

"Your mistress, then?" Piers said.

Blood suffused Almeida's face. "You delight in offending me, sir."

Piers sighed. "I would delight in the truth but it's like extracting blood from a stone. Did you fight a duel over the Condessa de Cartaxo? Perhaps with the conde."

"Cartaxo did not..." He broke off, looking hunted.

"Did not know?" April suggested. "What was his worst crime in your eyes?"

"*Crime*?" Almeida repeated. "He did not commit crime. He was a nobleman."

"A nobleman who supported the French," Piers pointed out.

"He did not support the French. He supported Portugal. He merely had different views as to the best way forward. He had long accepted the necessity of the British alliance."

For once, there seemed to be nothing insincere in Almeida's expression or voice, only impatience.

Piers changed tack. "Do you have business interests with the army, sir?"

"I do not," Almeida said with a hint of bitterness.

"How do you move your goods through the country or into Spain?"

"I don't," Almeida said, frowning. "Except by ship. When the goods land, they are someone else's problem. I am not a dashed merchant, sir."

Piers let that one go. He was pretty sure he had learned what he needed to, that Almeida had no obvious means to have set his minions on Bertie.

"May we speak to your wife?" he asked. "Please ask her to receive us."

Almeida struggled with outrage, but not for long.

Five minutes later, they were shown into the bare, cold drawing room, where Fortunata de Almeida greeted them with tea. Neither her husband nor her daughter was present.

"My husband tells me you have questions. Are they still about Major Withan?"

"They are," Piers said.

"You do not appear to have good fortune in finding him."

"Not so far," Piers agreed. "Were you aware of his attachment to your daughter?"

Fortunata stared at him for an instant, then burst into laughter. "My dear sir, I am not surprised you have not found poor Major Withan."

Piers smiled back amiably. "After you said your farewell to the major early on the evening before his departure, was that the last time you saw him?"

"I believe I said so."

"Would it surprise you to know he was in the grounds after eleven o'clock?"

Only the tiniest flicker of her eye betrayed her and that passed so quickly he almost missed it. She did know. And it annoyed her.

"Men will be men," she drawled. "He must have had a tryst with one of the maids. I forgive him, since he was going to war. It is certainly more likely than any tryst with my poor daughter. Who is about to contract a much more advantageous marriage."

"I wish her joy," Piers said blandly.

Chapter Twelve

"I don't like that house," April muttered, casting the Almeida residence a malevolent glance from the tree-lined street. "I'll bet their dead enemies are buried in the cellar. Your cousin's probably locked in the attic."

"He's very quiet if he is," Piers said.

"Do you think they're lying?"

He considered. "They're very good at it, aren't they?"

"Well, *she* is, the senhora. He lies as a matter of course but not very well. Eliana doesn't lie."

"Someone is lying," Lord Petteril said bleakly, "and we haven't yet found who."

"Maybe it's because we haven't talked to the right person yet. Like Captain Hood."

"I'm beginning to think you are right. Everett is too full of schoolboy honour to tell us the truth about his character. I wonder what his commanding officer thinks of him...."

"Then we're going with Captain Everett next week?" she asked, trying to keep the eagerness from her voice.

He regarded her speculatively. "I'm going to speak to a few people," he said at last.

"I've been thinking, too," April said. "How could no one have seen the major leaving the hotel with his trunk? There are always staff around early in the morning. And if the manager is so sure that he left then, why did he not ask for payment?"

"He never said he saw him leave," Petteril said thoughtfully. "He was relying on the word of the other staff, the invisible maids and porters. *You* speak to them, April. We've been concentrating too much on the night before he left rather than on the morning he did."

Accordingly, while Petteril walked round to the Envoy's office to see if he could find anyone who might tell him more about Captain Hood, April returned to their room and sent for the maid.

The girl, who must have been around her own age, arrived looking so frightened that April immediately felt guilty. Only a few months ago, her greatest ambition had been to work in some stables or other. Now she was terrifying respectable maids who would have been immeasurably above her.

It felt odd and unnatural, but she owed it to Lord Petteril to keep in character.

"I hope room is satisfactory, senhora," the girl said nervously.

"Oh, quite, quite. It's always clean and welcoming, which is why I know you must be a trustworthy person to talk to. What is your name?"

"Sabina, senhora."

"Sabina, you know my husband is looking for Major Withan?"

"Poor gentleman is missing, senhora. Bandidos," she said sadly. "Spaniards. Or French."

"You remember him then? Did you clean his room too?"

"No, senhora," Sabina replied, pointing above. "Rafaella."

"Could you ask her to come and speak to me?"

Sabina looked frightened. "No, senhora."

"No?" In spite of her new role as lady, April was startled.

"No, senhora. Rafaella does not work here anymore. She has a wonderful new job as housekeeper with a noble lady in the country."

"Does she...?" April's mind was spinning. "Do you know her address?"

"No, senhora. She was wanted very quickly. She said she would send to me but she has not."

"This noble lady would not be called Cartaxo, would she?"

"No, senhora. I cannot quite recall her name, but it was not that."

"Almeida?" April hazarded.

The girl brightened. "Yes! I believe it was...or at least something like that... No, wait," She straightened, beaming. "The Baroness de Campo Jacinto!"

April blinked but refrained from asking exactly how that was like Almeida. Instead, she asked, "Did you and Rafaella ever talk about Major Withan and his disappearance?"

"Sometimes," Sabina admitted. "We could not understand it, and he was so handsome, you could not help noticing him."

April, who had never found him handsome or remotely likeable, nodded sagely. "Of course. And you would be the ones who noticed most. When did Rafaella know he had left the hotel?"

"When his trunk was gone, before midday..." Sabina frowned. "But that was the odd thing. The major tell her he leave early in the morning, first light, so she decide to clean his room first and without knocking, she unlock it herself at about seven that morning. Then she flees, for his trunk is still there and she afraid he come out of the dressing closet and catch her! She goes back later, when she has cleaned the other rooms, and this time she knock! No answer, and now his trunk is gone."

"That is odd," April agreed, gazing at her, frowning. "So when Rafaella saw the trunk was still there, she didn't see the major himself? Could he have been still in bed?"

"No, the bed curtains were open but she not look very hard, just run out again in case she gets in trouble."

On impulse, April rose and took the major's abandoned bag from the wardrobe. "Do you recognize this?"

"Not really." Sabina raised her eyes from it to April's face. "Is it the major's? Rafaella found something like it under his bed when she was cleaning. As if he forgot it."

I don't think he forgot it at all. I think whoever took the trunk didn't know about the bag. The major was already gone...or dead.

PIERS RETURNED TO THE hotel late in the afternoon. While he asked questions about Captain Hood and stored away the answers, the back of his mind kept tormenting him with memories of Bertie, playing tricks, charming his way out of trouble, or hiding from it when there was no escape. Could Bertie really be hiding all this time? Deliberately destroyed his career in the army? If he hid, where in all the city—in the country—would he go?

Would he have got one of his women to hide him? Divina might have, but would Bertie really tolerate living in such squalor? Come to that, Piers couldn't see Lope tolerating it either, not once Bertie's money had run out. Which left the condessa and Senhora Almeida. And Eliana, of course. Eliana was the only one doing anything to find him. Was that because her mother knew where Bertie was? Did the condessa, the most self-contained of them all?

Somehow, he couldn't see the older women being so altruistic, and in any case, surely Bertie himself must know he couldn't hide forever.

Unless he had fled further afield, to the United States, perhaps, or Brazil...

It always came back to why.

"I've been talking to the maid, Sabina," April said, as soon as he entered the room. She poured him a glass of lemonade and left it on the table beside the armchair, while she spun around to the sofa and sat beside her notebook.

Gratefully, he threw off his coat and cravat and drank half the glassful in one gulp.

"The major's trunk didn't leave at dawn," April said. "The major might have left later with it, or he might never have come back from his adventures the night before. The maids never saw him. But seems to me the major wouldn't have forgotten his own bag—which the maid found abandoned under the bed."

"Not unless he was injured," Piers said slowly. "And he went into hiding."

"Do you think that's likely?" April asked.

"As likely as any other theory at this point," Piers said.

April frowned, "There's definitely something strange going on. Rafaella, the maid who cleaned the major's room, was suddenly offered a wonderful new position with a noblewoman in the country and left immediately. As if she was got out of the way before she could tell anyone about seeing Bertie's trunk after he was supposed to have left Lisbon."

Piers frowned, laying down his glass. "The trunk gives the lie to the theory he left the city. Even Bertie would not be hours late for a military expedition."

"Could he have ordered the trunk to be sent after him?" April suggested.

"Why? There were pack animals to carry the baggage. The trunk was already packed and ready to go. Which noblewoman took the maid?"

"A baroness..." April consulted her notebook. "De Campo Jacinto. Impoverished, elderly lady, apparently, desperate for a new housekeeper. And Raffaella was desperate for the promotion. She hasn't communicated since leaving. I think we need to find her."

Piers nodded. "I think we probably do. We never seem to get any closer, do we?"

"Did you discover anything about Captain Hood?"

"That he had a temper, could be vindictive, and had something of a chip on his shoulder about nobleman's sons with no experience being promoted over his head."

"Not quite as Everett described him, then," April said, frowning as she scribbled this information into her book. "But would he have been so stupid as to leave Bertie alone? Is he not in trouble for this?"

"His claim is that Bertie never left Lisbon. That at no time did Hood ever catch sight of him, despite riding back more than once, so he knew he wasn't coming."

"And he just accepted that? Because he despised inexperienced gen-tlemen soldiers promoted over his head? His guv...*superiors* accepted this?"

Piers's lips twitched. In spite of everything, her occasional lapses in speech were endearing. "It's possible Hood had no objection what-ever to Bertie getting in trouble for his laxness. The general feeling about Hood seems to be that an experienced soldier like him would not have left a man exposed—even one who stole his women and had been promoted over him. And frankly, even if Hood was foolish enough to—er... croak Bertie, how could he have managed it without the other soldiers with him knowing?"

"Perhaps they did. Perhaps it's a huge conspiracy. Or... You said he rode back a couple of times to look for signs of the major. If he went alone, he could have done it then."

"Which brings us back to why. There are enough people dying in this war without dirtying one's hands with murder of one's own. None of it makes sense." He rose to his feet. "Let's go and find something to eat, get a good night's sleep and start again early tomorrow."

The days were passing too fast. It chilled him, almost panicked him, for if Bertie hadn't been dead when they arrived in Lisbon, he could be by now. More than a month had passed since he had last been seen. Piers was running out of time.

DESPITE THE BEST INTENTIONS, when they returned to the hotel, Piers took April's notebook out onto the balcony, and read everything she had written about the search for Bertie. The heat of the day was less intense, and it was a pleasant spot in which to read and think. These were the things he was supposed to be good at.

If Bertie was just the victim of bad luck, of some villain in Lisbon's back streets, why had anyone troubled to remove his trunk?

Was any pursuit of Rafaella the maid and her exotically named new mistress, the baroness, a waste of time? This, and the route to Cuidad Rodrigo, were the only things left to investigate. They had to reveal the truth...

Except Piers could not quite rid his mind of the notion that he had already had the truth and he just wasn't seeing it. Some connection was not forming in his brain as it should.

He took some unintended time to admire April's writing and her turn of phrase, as well as her sharp observations, conscious of a glow of pride that wasn't terribly helpful to the problem in hand. But then, sometimes he thought best when he just let his mind wander where it would, over phrases and ideas.

His mind drifted off, building up possibilities as far as they would go with the facts, encountering impenetrable objects, taking a step back to a different path and moving forward until that theory was blocked, too. From the chaotic drifting, which served to sharpen his memory, his mind had turned methodical, forming and discarding ideas from the events of Bertie's last known evening in Lisbon, and the morning he should have left, placing all the players in their scenes with their characters and motivations. Especially Bertie's.

Darkness fell at some point. April did not disturb him, although he was vaguely aware of her moving in the room behind him. She spoke once and he nodded as though he heard her, her presence a mere pleasant, even necessary backdrop to everything in his head.

Gradually, it all got jumbled in his tired brain and he fell asleep in his chair with the smell of the sea blotting out the less pleasant stench of the city, reminding him of the shipboard journey.

He woke with a start and knew.

"Your cousin's probably locked in the attic." April's words outside the Almeida's house echoed in his head, repeating into the distance.

It was still dark. Rising, he stumbled through the balcony door into the room. April had left a lamp burning low and by its light he could see her small huddle under the bed sheet. So vulnerable beneath her brave impudence and forceful embracing of life. But even that didn't matter right now.

"April," he said, and at once her head lifted from the pillow. "I know what happened. I know where Bertie is."

DUARTE DE ALMEIDA WOKE in the condessa's bed for what he knew would be the last time.

He should not have come. He hadn't really wanted to, and if he was honest with himself, he doubted Beatriz cared very much whether he was there or not. His wife cared. He was returning to a much more positive affection for Fortunata, her loyalty and smart good sense.

Beatriz did not stir. She always slept the sleep of the righteous, even in adultery, even in guilty widowhood. Almeida had stopped sleeping well a month ago. Everything worried him too much, from his own dwindling wealth to the English officer... But all would come right now.

Dressed, he sat by the window to wait for enough light in the sky to leave without being seen in any clarity.

FORTUNATA DE ALMEIDA knew her husband was with Beatriz de Cartaxo. She rather thought it would be the last time and was pleased. Not because she truly loved Duarte anymore, but one had one's pride.

Lying in bed, wakeful before the dawn, she found herself wishing there had been a way, just once, to lie with the English officer with the passionate, sensual mouth and the laughing eyes. Duarte had never looked at her like that.

And poor Major Withan was dead.

But she had found a way to revive their fortunes. She and Duarte and Eliana would survive and prosper.

ELIANA WAS ALREADY up, staring out of the window at the first creeping of dawn into the sky. In a little while, she would see her father sneaking back into the house, but neither she nor her mother would mention it.

Eliana could not stomach such a marriage. Even if Major Withan had not disappeared, she knew his affection for her would not have lasted. He had found her different and appealing, and she would always be grateful to him for that. It was why she was so eager to help the other Englishman, Whittey, to find him. But even if he did, even if the major came back, men like him did not marry girls like her, except on impulse— which she, as much as he, would regret when he began to stray.

And now her parents had told her of this next ridiculous marriage idea—to the major's cousin the viscount! No, the nunnery beckoned Eliana. If only she could know the major was safe.

A man was sneaking through the gate—always left unlocked by her father—but it was not the master of the house. It was a servant of some kind, not one of theirs, and he carried a letter in his hand. He vanished from her view, then a few moments later, trotted back the way he had come.

Intrigued, Eliana went downstairs and discovered the letter on the hall floor. It was addressed to her.

CAPTAIN EVERETT WAS not best pleased to be woken by thunderous knocking on the lodging house door. Since he was on the ground floor of the building, he pulled on his breeches, left his room and limped across the hall to open the door and scowl at the perpetrator.

"Good morning," said Whittey the Foreign Officer investigator cheerfully. "Want to come and fetch Bertie Withan?"

Everett felt his blood run cold.

BEATRIZ, CONDESSA DE Cartaxo, woke with the knowledge that Duarte had just let himself out of her bedchamber. She doubted he would be back and was glad of it. God preserve her from stupid and ineffectual men. Recently, she had only accepted him to annoy Fortunata, whom she could not bear.

Once, she had thought Major Withan might be different.

No point in thinking of him now. Oddly, it was the other Englishman, Whittey, who popped into her mind. He pretended to be a little stupid and a little ineffectual, but he was not. One could see it in his quizzical eyes, in the unexpected firmness of his chin.

Withan, she thought, reaching over to pull the bell for her maid, sounded a lot like Whittey. In fact, now she thought of it, was there not some familiarity in the shape of Whittey's face? In the lean contours of his bones and his long, surely aristocratic nose?

Her stomach clenched. Without pulling the bell rope, she drew back her arm and sat up as suspicion dawned.

Recognizing that Whittey was more than he seemed, she had still never suspected what he actually was. In fact, she still didn't know, but she began to believe that he was rather closer to the major than anyone had told her. Which meant that he would try harder and upset her plans if he could.

He was not immune to her charms. She had seen appreciation in his eyes. The man liked beauty. It might even be amusing in its own right to take him from his pretty, curious little wife.

She reached again for the bell, just as the imperious knocking began on the front door.

Chapter Thirteen

When the thundering began on the condessa's front door, Almeida was halfway across the entrance hall.

He had been moving discreetly toward the side door where his egress was less likely to be observed by servants. Not that the condessa's servants were ever unaware of his presence. She was well protected day and night, as was proved now by the fact that a manservant stepped out of his porter's box by the front door, presumably to give such lamentably early callers short shrift.

Not by a twitch of a whisker did the servant betray that he had seen Almeida. And Almeida, poised to dart down the passage to the side door, elected to stay where he was after all. Curiosity was inevitable in such circumstances, and it was past time to look after his own interests.

So, he stayed where he was, even turned his head slightly to pick up every word before the servant closed the door in their faces.

But it was a very peremptory voice that spoke in heavily accented Portuguese. "The condessa if you please. Please convey our respects and apologies to the lady and explain that our commission is a matter of great urgency and importance to both our countries. Here is my card."

The servant, keeping the door open a mere crack, took the card proffered by the unseen hand and gazed at it for some time, as though uncertain. But, like all the condessa's people, the servant was well trained, and Almeida had no expectation that the insolent caller would be admitted.

What Almeida had not allowed for was the unexpected. Though holding the door in place, the servant turned to Almeida.

"Senhor? Should I admit them and wake her excellency?" As he spoke, he held out the card in Almeida's direction, unable to leave his post to present it as he should.

Almeida, petrified of being seen, almost bolted, but since the servant was still in place, he crossed the hall obliquely and snatched the card from his fingers.

Jonathan Jeffery, Esq. Secretary to the British Envoy Extraordinaire to Portugal.

Possibly, Almeida's alarm was written on his face. Since his recent encounters with Whittey, he wanted nothing to do with the Envoy's staff. But something distracted the servant from his guard duty, for suddenly the door pushed open and an alarming number of people spilled through.

For the first time in months, Almeida rose to the occasion.

"Inform the condessa," he instructed the servant. "I shall remain with her guests until we receive her commands. Gentlemen, please follow me."

Since their call was untimely and they were very unlikely to be received, he did not take them to the condessa's private sitting room, but to the nearest reception room, where he invited them coldly to sit. He did not offer refreshment. He wanted them to be well aware of their ill manners.

Only then did he examine his guests. The speaker, he of the card, he knew only by sight. Another was the Envoy's fellow who had been present at his wife's most recent reception. Calvin? Kelvin? One was a British army officer with a limp whom Fortunata had made something of a pet of during his recovery from a serious wound. Captain Everett? Whittey, he recognized with loathing, wearing a rather threadbare traveling cloak against the early morning chill.

They sat in silence, which Almeida felt no compulsion to break. He rather looked forward to following their hostess's orders and escorting them from the house, perhaps with a civil message to call again in a few hours, perhaps not.

Beatriz, bless her, obviously meant her visitors to sweat for their ill manners, for her response was not immediate. The silence stretched out some fifteen minutes before, much to Almeida's surprise, the condessa herself swept into the room.

She was dressed perfectly and modestly in widow's black, a further rebuke to the rudeness of her visitors, who at least all rose and bowed to her.

She did not offer her hand, although she greeted them all by name, including Almeida —as though he had entered with them, which he thought a nice touch of discretion. Then her eyes darted around the room as though looking for someone else. Was she being sarcastic?

"Where is Senhora Whittey?" she asked.

"Condessa?" Almeida asked, startled.

"I am told you gentlemen arrived with a lady," Beatriz said coldly, and yet for the first time ever, Almeida saw something very like fear in her beautiful eyes. "In which case, *where is she?*"

IN FACT, APRIL HAD entered the house with Lord Petteril, at the back of their little train of visitors. While the porter shot off to the back of the house to convey his message, and Almeida stalked ahead of the visitors to a reception room, April veered away and ran lightly up the stairs.

It was all part of their plan – albeit a part Petteril had objected to until he realized that she was the best person to remain unnoticed for longest. Knowing the condessa's guests were never left alone for an instant, she had skulked at the back of the throng outside the door. Even so, the servant had clocked her. She didn't think Almeida had, though she half expected a hue and cry after her as she bolted upward.

Her goal was the attic, in particular the room with the shutters that were never open. Both she and Petteril had noticed this during each visit, but the condessa's house was hardly the bordello. She had genteel neighbours and an army of servants. A man would have been impossible to hide, especially a man surely imprisoned against his will.

"Would he?" Petteril had said to her in the darkness. He had forgotten himself so far that he had actually sat on the edge of her bed to tell her his theory. "Her servants are nearly all men, such that what maids there are rush to obey them. None of them says a word out of turn and they escort visitors very carefully from the front door to the condessa and back again. Even the gardener couldn't wait to be rid of you when you were praising his work."

"But the house is hardly the criminal backstreets of the city! The major would yell, make a racket the world was bound to hear! Unless he *wanted* to be hidden?"

She had a mere impression of Petteril's violent shake of the head. "No. The condessa has easy access to medical supplies, remember? There was ether in that crate I fell over outside her warehouse. Also known as sweet oil of vitriol when mixed with alcohol and water. Some of my friends in Oxford larked about with it at one time. So did I. She'll have opium of some kind, too, all means of keeping Bertie unconscious and quiet."

"For a month?" April had said incredulously.

"God knows what state he is in," Petteril had answered.

April trusted his judgement, but she could not suppress the niggling feeling that in this he was wrong. He wanted to believe in his cousin's survival too much. April was more inclined to believe that it was the major's body hidden in that room while the condessa awaited her opportunity to be rid of it. No doubt she masked the smell in a coffin-like box.

On the first landing, April almost came to grief as a maid with her hair askew bolted along from the other direction. April only just managed to flatten herself on the stairs before the woman almost burst through the door on her left. Presumably, this was the condessa's maid, summoned with urgency.

April and Petteril had both agreed that the condessa would be unlikely to throw them out. If his theory was correct—and April suspected most of it was—the condessa would want to know what they knew, what they wanted with her at such an unseemly hour. To say nothing of wishing to be seen to offer all possible co-operation.

As soon as the condessa's bedchamber door closed, April jumped up and ran for the next flight of stairs. Halfway up, where they could not be seen from below, they narrowed spectacularly, leading to a locked door.

April, whose skills seemed to have been honed rather than wilted by association with Lord Petteril—they had always earned her a smack from criminal confederates—picked the lock in no time and was through to a narrow passage. There was not much daylight, but a lamp of some kind showed a door at the other end of this short passage, perhaps to servants' quarters and a servants' staircase.

April hurried along, dropping her lock picks back into the bag hidden beneath her cloak. Growing used the gloom, she saw that the light came from another short passage on her left. This, surely, was about the right place for the constantly shuttered window.

She turned into the passage, and immediately sprang back again. A man was seated on a hard wooden chair outside a closed door, the only door there. He was large, as all the condessa's manservants seemed to be, his head resting back against the wall.

From the opposite end of the first passage came a shout. April only had time to fall through an open door before the other door to the servants' quarters flew open.

"Goncalo!" a manservant shouted from there, and the seated man in the left-hand passage lumbered around the corner. The summoner must have gone back the way he came, for Goncalo followed him, calling. The far door closed and locked.

Taking her chance for whatever few moments she was given, April flew out of hiding, bolted around the corner to the door that had been guarded. A quick push at the latch told her it was locked.

Ramming her ear against the wood, she listened, and heard nothing.

Dead, she thought, with pity for Lord Petteril. Yet why guard a dead man?

She scratched softly at the door. "Major," she hissed. "Major Withan?"

Unsurprisingly, no sound came from within.

"Major," she tried again, with even less hope. "I've come from Lord Petteril."

Her breath caught, for surely something rustled inside?

"Major," she said with more urgency, delving back into her bag for her lock picks. "Is it you? I'm going to try and unlock the door, but I don't think I've got long and I can't carry you. Are you well?"

"It's a trick," came a hoarse, weak voice in English. "I still won't tell you."

"Just tell me if you can walk," April responded, inserting one prong into the lock and then the other.

"I can stumble along with the worst," said the English voice. It didn't sound much like Petteril's Cousin Bertie. It slurred words like a drunk and it was dull, without arrogance or hope. "Go away."

"Ungrateful bastard," April said, reverting to type more by instinct that thought.

Certainly, it seemed to have an effect, for something creaked, like an old bed when someone sits up.

"If you've got boots or shoes, put them on," she ordered, manipulating the lock. Her tool slipped and she tried again, forcing herself to concentrate.

"Only stockings and they're somewhat ripe." This sounded more like Major Withan, though conversely, she had the impression he wasn't really sure what he was saying. "You sound like..."

"Oh, I am and he's waiting for you downstairs."

"I don't believe you!" he shouted with such despair that April actually knew a surge of pity.

At the same time, the lock clicked open, someone yelled from the servants' end of the passage, accompanied by pounding feet. April had nowhere to run. There was no time to bolt back to her previous hiding place.

She could just run, leap over the banisters if necessary, as she had often enough before. Lord Petteril and safety lay below, and she knew Major Withan was here, exactly as he had said.

Only Petteril wouldn't want his cousin left alone longer than he needed to be. The poor s...*gentleman* needed help. She whisked herself into his prison and shut the door behind her.

Major Albert Withan, Bertie to his family and friends, sat on a truckle bed in a crumpled shirt, pantaloons and stockinged feet. On his jaw and chin, so similar in shape to Lord Petteril's and yet so different in strength, grew at least a couple of days' stubble, lending him a grubby, unkempt appearance only enhanced by the spiky, tangled hair which had grown longer than he usually allowed. The skin around his cavernous, bloodshot eyes looked bruised from exhaustion.

The mattress on the bed was bare save for a solitary blanket. There was no furniture in the room, although, bizarrely, a trunk lay open at the foot of the bed. There didn't seem to be much in it. The window was shut and shuttered. The room smelled of stale air, sweat, human waste and something unpleasantly chemical.

The major stared at her, his shaking hands gripping each other in his lap.

He laughed. "I knew it was a trick!"

"It's me," April said urgently, batting dismissively at her skirts. "April, Ape, his lordship's assistant. You know, you've met me."

He squeezed his eyes shut. "I'll tell you nothing!"

"Don't want to hear anything yet. They're coming, Major." She took hold of his trembling hand, and he was so astonished, his jaw dropped. She grinned at him. "He's waiting below, too, so go ahead and yell. Ready?"

As the servants barged along the corridor, she began to scream and shout. And after a stunned moment, the major joined in, yelling at the top of his voice, which seemed suddenly stronger with hope.

As the men threw themselves against the door and into the room, he stopped, uttering in despair. "They'll gas us both!"

"Not this time!" she cried and raised her voice in a blaze of triumph against those who had held him so cruelly for so long. And with a sob, Bertie Withan joined in again.

The three menservants who broke into the room seemed momentarily disconcerted, One held an ill-smelling cloth. The others lunged at the major, April jumped up, kicked and punched them. One seized her by the hair, but she didn't stop, merely lashed out at the man with the cloth and kept yelling.

And then a voice spoke over the top of the din. In Portuguese and then again in English, a haughty voice commanded, "*Para!* Stop."

The viscount had entered and the cold fury in his face and voice could have toppled governments. Behind him, loads of people piled into the tiny room—Jeffery and Kelvin, Almeida, Everett, the condessa. And yet for an instant, silence reigned.

The servants had released the major. Across the tension, Lord Petteril and his cousin stared at each other.

"Piers," whispered Bertie, tears starting to his eyes. He seemed to have no other words. "Piers." He tried to stumble to his feet, but Petteril was quicker, already sitting on the bed beside him, holding him like a baby.

"Yes, me again, never quite shaken off," he said lightly. Probably only April heard the near break in his voice, the emotion he hadn't expected and didn't want. "Thought it was time you came home."

Major Withan, the arrogant bully who had once despised and stolen from his cousin, grasped him like a lifeline and could not speak.

Over his head, Petteril met the condessa's resigned gaze. "Downstairs, I think. Everyone out while I see to my cousin's comfort."

The condessa's eyebrows flew up. "*Cousin?*"

A few other jaws had dropped, too.

Without a further word, the condessa spun around in a swirl of silk and led the way out. The large manservants followed obediently. Almeida, his mouth open in astonishment as he stared at Bertie, was dragged out by Kelvin and Jeffery.

April herded the last of them out of the room and followed, closing the door on the cousins. She scowled at everyone because Lord Petteril was so wonderful she wanted to cry.

IF, AT THE WORST OF his boyhood pain of humiliation and rejection, Piers had ever dreamed of being the one who was turned to when true strength was needed, the one who saved his brother and his cousins from trouble they had got themselves into, he could no longer remember it. There was only the shock of Bertie's physical weakness, the trembling body and the shattered confidence.

There was no question of Bertie not being pleased to be seen by him in such a state. Bertie grasped the familiar, the known. Piers's fierce anger at what had been done to him was laced with helpless pity.

He was relieved when the vice-like grip on his hand relaxed and Bertie sat up. "It's the shock," he said hoarsely. "How did you find me?"

"We talked to everyone and I thought about it. I'm sorry it took so long."

Bertie actually laughed, a shaky but definite effort. "Don't. You'll set me off again."

"What happened? How did you end up here like this?"

"Cartaxo. The conde. There was something about him I could not like." He began very faintly, as if unused to speaking, but gradually, as the words poured out of him like ale from a jug, his voice grew stronger.

"I put it down to the fact that I knew his history of supporting the French, though he was growing increasingly close to the current Portuguese government and courting the British, surrounding himself with soldiers and diplomats. Then, by chance, I saw him in the back streets, where he had no business to be. I followed him, heard him speaking in French to someone else—telling him somewhere the British planned to attack and with what force.

"I challenged him. Who wouldn't? He was a gentleman. I expected some explanation that I could believe in—that he was feeding the French false information, or the Frenchman was on our side. But he admitted the Frenchman was a spy, told me with unbearable superiority that I had no say in his country's future and that beside his greatness no one would believe me, a mere rattle-pated soldier, newly arrived in the country. I had just made a play for his wife, so he was probably right. So I did the only thing left to me. I called him out."

The only thing? A quiet word with his commanding officer, with Sir Charles Stuart or even his underlings would have managed the matter much more effectively. But Bertie had probably felt very alone, part of something important for the first time in his life. He was trying to do the right thing.

"You didn't tell anyone about the duel, but there was still a whisper of it," Piers murmured.

"Cartaxo claimed to be too busy to meet me for several days, until the night before I was due to leave Lisbon, in fact. He insisted on night time, indoors in a deserted fencing school—I think he owned it—without seconds, since the charge was so shaming. I allowed it. I was always pretty useful at fencing, thought the victory would be easy. I insisted that if I won, we should go to the authorities—his and mine—with what I had overheard. He agreed, probably because I had thus signed my own death warrant."

"So, you met him late on the night before you were supposed to leave," Piers said.

"There was no duel," Bertie said flatly. "He tried to murder me as soon as I entered the place. Almost succeeded, too." Bertie raised his gaze from his hands to Piers's face. "I had to kill him. It was the only way to stop him killing me. And the only way to stop what he was doing. You do see that, don't you?"

"I do see that," Piers allowed, although he saw several other ways too. They were not Bertie's ways. "What then?"

"I was still wondering what to do with the body when the condessa came in with her entourage of brutes. She seemed remarkably calm for a woman who had just been widowed, and believe me, there was a lot of blood. She issued a stream of orders I could not understand. Half the men took Cartaxo's body away. The other half overpowered me with the aid of some chemical on a filthy rag that I was forced to breathe in till I lost consciousness."

Piers drew in his breath. "Can you bear to tell the rest before witnesses? It will clear you both with the Portuguese and with the army. I brought Everett as well as fellows from the Envoy's staff."

"You think of everything," Bertie said with a lopsided smile that for once seemed to mock himself rather than Piers. "There's a lot to be said for brains. I don't suppose there's a coat still in that trunk?"

Chapter Fourteen

April gave the condessa her due. She did not even try to escape. Nor did her menservants who were herded into a corner of her beautiful sitting room with Everett pointing a pistol at them. April sent a maid scuttling to fetch Dado, who had been watching the back doors with a couple of friends in case of any attempt to smuggle the major out. He came in now and leaned negligently against the wall beside the door.

The condessa made no effort to have him removed.

In fact, the Condessa de Cartaxo was rather magnificent in her own way. Ignoring the guarded men and her guards, she ordered breakfast for her uninvited guests.

"I don't understand," Jeffery said at last. "How did you keep him here for an entire *month*? How could you keep such a thing secret?"

"Frightened servants, loyal and presumably well-paid bravos," April said contemptuously. "And a lot of ether. She could have killed him."

The condessa shrugged. "It was difficult to move him somewhere quieter. By the time I had sorted out my husband's affairs, questions about the major's disappearance had begun. When *they* died down, this Whittey begins again." She met April's gaze. "I beg your pardon, viscondessa. This *Lord Petteril* begins again."

"He is really Lord Petteril?" Kelvin said uneasily, thinking, no doubt, of his none too respectful manners towards the lowly Whittey.

Everyone looked at April. Almeida, clearly remembering the letter he had so recently sent to his lordship, showed the glimmerings of fear in his appalled expression.

"He is the viscount," April said.

"I never knew he was married," Almeida said miserably.

"He must care a lot for his cousin to do this in person," Jeffery said.

"Somewhat underhanded," Almeida snapped.

April stared at him in disbelief, and at least he had the grace to blush. "As the junior Mr. Whittey he was able to ask more questions of more people, without inspiring huge ransom demands. You take my point, senhor?"

It was quite fun playing the viscountess. She wasn't sure she liked the way everyone's manner changed towards her, but life was all about appearances. If they knew she was, in fact, a thief from the gutters of St. Giles, she would be shown the door—the kitchen door—and never allowed back in. Such was life.

Conversation lapsed again, everyone looking furtively at everyone else, until Lord Petteril and Major Withan walked slowly into the room. Petteril, without the cloak he had arrived in, was dressed as the viscount in his well-tailored finery with his quizzing glasses dangling from their ribbons around his neck, had given his cousin his arm. April thought he needed it. The major, still unshaven but in a clean shirt and slightly crumpled plain coat, had combed his hair and looked a bit cleaner. He still seemed slightly dazed but at least an echo of the old arrogance was trying to reappear.

Jeffery immediately rose to give the major his armchair nearest the door. Lord Petteril stood beside him. And since no one really wanted to look at the poor major whom, in some way, they had all let down, everyone gazed expectantly at his lordship.

Lord Petteril drew in his breath to speak—and a sudden altercation in the hallway beyond distracted him and everyone else. Two raised female voices could be heard and then, abruptly, the door flew open and Eliana de Almeida stalked into the room.

The men all sprang to their feet, even her father. "Eliana!" he exclaimed, then rattled off a question in Portuguese which April easily translated as, "What the devil are you doing here?"

Eliana, ignored him, her gaze darting around the room until she found the major. Somehow, he had stumbled to his feet unaided, and swayed beside Petteril, white-faced, staring at her.

Her anxious gaze drank him in, his appearance and his condition. Her eyes flashed, immediately lighting up her plain face with a joy that was beauty in itself. Ignoring her father, she ran straight to Bertie Withan, who seized both her hands and kissed them passionately, one after the other.

Over their heads, April met Petteril's gaze and raised her eyebrows. *See? I told you.*

His lips twitched. The slightest of graceful shrugs acknowledged her point.

The couple meanwhile were exchanging a stream of broken-voiced words in mangled English and Portuguese.

Petteril interrupted, moving aside and placing a chair for Eliana next to his cousin's. Almeida looked outraged, his mouth opening and closing with thwarted fury. With Petteril's bland gaze upon him, it seemed he could not speak. Everyone sat down again.

"How kind of Senhorita de Almeida to join us," Petteril said, again looking directly at April who smiled sunnily because she was the one who had written to Eliana telling her to come here as early as she could for news of the major. "Since we have at least representatives of all interested parties present, shall we begin explanations? Why, Condessa? Or shall I guess?"

The condessa waved one graceful hand. "Your guesses appear to be good. I always knew you were clever, but you are a subtler man than I gave you credit for. However, I am not so lacking in courage that I will not claim my own mistakes. And they are many, beginning with my marriage."

"You claim your own mistakes by blaming them on your husband?" Eliana threw the words across the room at her.

The condessa eyed her speculatively. "Not all of them. I chose him after all. My parents merely obeyed me. Most people do. To the point. Severino, my husband the conde, as everyone knows, chose to welcome the French. For what it is worth, I agreed with him at the time, and at first we did very well, socially and financially. But, believe it or not, I am a patriot. I believe in the freedom of Portugal. Severino remained devoted to his French ideals and when the British alliance was formed to kick out the French, I could do little more than persuade him to arm both sides with guns and medicines."

"I believe you still did very well, socially and financially," Petteril said politely.

She shrugged. "I used my brain. Severino paid increasingly less attention to his. He used his position, growing increasingly closer to government, to glean information which he passed on to the French. I could not stop him since if he fell, so did I. You curl your lip at me, viscondessa," she said, looking suddenly at April. "I don't imagine you have ever faced prison or execution."

April laughed.

Slightly disconcerted, the condessa blinked and returned her gaze to Petteril, who seemed now to be the only person in the room she acknowledged.

"Like most fools, Severino was convinced of his own cleverness. When he allowed himself to be overheard by Major Withan, passing his information to his favourite French spy, he imagined he could silence him. He manipulated the major into challenging him to a duel—alone at night in his fencing school. It was not clever, major, to agree to such a meeting."

Bertie muttered something under his breath.

"I did not see what happened next," the condessa proceeded, "though I can guess. I imagine Severino immediately attacked Major

Withan to murder him. By the time I found him, he certainly bore a few cuts and bruises. My husband, however, came off worse. Much worse. When I arrived, he lay quite dead in a pool of his own blood."

Almeida uttered an exclamation of horror and pity. The condessa's glance at him contained largely contempt.

"I had my servants remove the body. And the major. You will appreciate I could not have him running loose around Lisbon, accusing my husband—and therefore me—of treason and attempted murder."

"By dawn, he would have left Lisbon," Petteril pointed out.

"But still talking," the condessa snapped. She sat back. "Besides, there was the matter of his wounds to treat."

"Such mercy," marvelled the viscount. "There was also, of course, the matter of how much he knew and how far he could implicate you."

"I did not much care about that." Her lips curved into a sardonic smile. "I am a mere woman, dependent on my husband. What I needed from Major Withan, was information to buy back the favour of the government and the British, should Severino's treason ever come to light. And of course, I needed the major not to talk to anyone else."

"So you kept him here bound and drugged for over a month?" Jeffery said in outrage. "You allowed his family and friends to think him dead? You tried to destroy a human being!"

The condessa shrugged. "You dramatize. He was drugged only when he tried to make noise, bound only because he tried to escape. When he gave me his promise to be silent and not to escape, I gave him mine not to bind him or drug him. He is fed, he is cared for and free."

"Free to wander that vast room you kept him in, without light or even bedlinen?"

"He tried to escape using the bed linen."

The major himself interrupted this exchange, frowning at the condessa. "Your questions were to find out about the French spies to warn the government? Why did you not tell me that? Of course I told you nothing." He blinked twice and actually laughed. "You even suggested

I marry you! Think of all that wealth, Piers. I'd have never had to touch you for the readies ever again."

A tinge of colour seeped into the condessa's face. "If you are married to me, you do not tell things against me. And I have a husband respectable to the allies. But you are too stubborn, I don't know what to do with you."

"Well, you never tried to kill me," Bertie allowed. "Though I suspect you were about to move me to the country to do just that."

"Don't be stupid. I could not kill you. We were going to my house in the country until you saw sense."

"We looked there," April remarked.

"Well, if you had not come here asking your questions, you would have found him there," the condessa retorted. "Now you all know everything, shall we have breakfast?"

She rose to her feet, disarmingly the perfect hostess. But Captain Everett spoke from the corner, his pistol still pointed at the menservants.

"Wait. We don't know everything at all. What did you do with the conde's body? How did he end up outside the bordello?"

The condessa stared at him, and then began to laugh.

"Because the conde owned the building," Lord Petteril said. "It was his wife's little revenge for his betrayals, both personal and public. As his widow, the condessa could ruin his reputation only so far without harming herself. This way, she won sympathy but no suspicion. Her own private joke, I daresay."

"You really are quite clever, aren't you?" she said, an edge to her voice.

"No," Petteril replied modestly. "Actually, you left us all the clues. It took me too long to put them together and remove all the confusion."

"More than we managed," Jeffery muttered.

"And the ruffians who attacked us in the street?" Captain Everett pursued.

"The condessa's, I imagine," Petteril said without much interest, waving a vague hand toward her menservants herded in the corner. "She didn't want too many questions asked so tried to scare us off with a little violence. Or at least the threat of it."

The condessa did not deny it. "I am going to breakfast," she said, sailing across the room. "You are welcome to join me."

Everyone looked at Piers, who waved one hand ironically in front of him. "You must all do as you see fit now that you have the facts. I have no authority here. Bertie, your carriage awaits. The condessa will no doubt send on your things."

Something that wasn't quite laughter caught in April's throat. It struck her that the condessa was a little like his lordship, focused and clever and untroubled by convention, seeking her own path by whatever means at her disposal. But something was lacking in her, something that April would always be wary of. It reminded her too much of St. Giles.

She returned the condessa's gracious nod with one rather more curt and preceded both Withans across the hall and out the front door into the blessedly fresh morning air. Once there, she was reluctant to enter the carriage. She wanted to walk home, away from everyone, even *him*.

But it was Lord Petteril who, as though understanding, blocked her escape and handed her firmly into the carriage. She didn't fight him. She had to help with Bertie, whom she drew down beside her on the front facing bench. Petteril sat opposite them and when the horses started off, leaned forward, not to his cousin, but to her.

He touched her cheek. "Your face is cut. Your arm is bruised."

She blinked before the concern in his eyes.

"She fought like a tigress, Piers," Major Withan said shakily. "For me. She doesn't even like me."

A smile entered Lord Petteril's eyes, warm, concerned and unbearably kind. "That's my girl," he said softly, like balm to her soul.

MAJOR WITHAN WAS GIVEN his own room at the hotel, with the beaming pleasure of the manager. Lemonade, wine, water and a light breakfast were sent up to his room, and April sat with him while Lord Petteril went to call on the Envoy and arrange for doctors to be sent to the major and news of his adventures to his commanding officers in Spain.

With the windows thrown wide to the sun, the major sat in silence. His fingers still trembled slightly as he raised his glass to his lips, but his face bore an oddly tranquil expression. April did not disturb his thoughts.

He said abruptly, "I couldn't bear the stuff on that cloth. I promised silence to avoid it. I never dreamed it would go on so long. I'd no idea how much time passed. Was that cowardly of me? Should I have kept trying to fight?"

"No. They would always have overpowered you, drugged you."

Major Withan started, as though he had forgotten someone else was in the room. His desperately pale face flushed, and he lapsed again into silence and his own thoughts.

Then he frowned. "He came out here to find me. *Piers* did."

"He will always come and get you," April said, echoing the words his lordship had once said to her. Something in her heart twisted, because she spoke the truth. Lord Petteril's kindness extended far and wide. She was his friend, but the major was family. He had room for both in his large, unconventional heart and April admired him all the more for it. Still, a tiny part of her wished to be the only special one. "He came and got me, too, more than once. I go and get him when he needs me to."

Bertie shifted his gaze to her a little too quickly. There might have been shame in his eyes. Certainly, there was thought.

Then he said, "You came with him to find me."

I will always go with him.

THE FOLLOWING MORNING, quite early while the city was still cool and quietish, Piers conducted April down the steps from the hotel.

"How is he?" she asked.

A carriage had pulled up in front of the hotel. A middle-aged lady in regal lilac, who had just alighted, was gazing toward them, or perhaps the hotel's front door, while she awaited her fellow passengers.

"Much better," Piers replied. "He wanted to come down alone, testing himself with normality, I think."

After bathing, shaving and dressing in borrowed clothes, Bertie had spent the previous day on their balcony, dozing and talking, eating a little and appreciating the world and his companions in a manner his cousin would never have imagined when he began this search.

The night had been harder. Piers had spent it uncomfortably on a truckle bed in Bertie's room, listening to his cousin's restless tossing and turning, interspersed with short, disturbed sleeps, and occasional sobbing breaths.

But as the light filtered through the un-shuttered window, Bertie had risen with pleasure, a glimmer of his old self in his eyes, and suggested going out to have a gentle breakfast.

"Eliana might join us," he had said, which Piers repeated now to April.

"Is he serious about her?" she asked.

"Possibly. Hard to tell while he's in this state, grateful to anyone who didn't forget him. I think he likes her because she is different from his usual flirts. Time will tell if there's more to it. His main problem will be convincing her not to go into a nunnery while he makes up his mind. And preventing her parents from marrying her off to some rich old nonentity."

"Like you?" April asked, grinning cheekily.

"Not rich enough," Piers said. "Besides, even Almeida couldn't stomach me as his son-in-law."

The family from the carriage were sailing toward the front door of the hotel, but as though she had just seen him, the lady in lilac veered toward them, wreathed in smiles, dragging a younger lady, possibly her daughter, in her wake.

"Why, what a surprise to find you here! How do you do? I don't believe you know my daughter Margaret?"

"I don't believe I do," Piers said, having no idea who the devil the mother was either. The haughty viscount bowed distantly to both ladies and threaded April's hand into the crook of his arm. He would have walked away, only the lady seemed only just to have noticed April.

April looked particularly pretty in her sunny, yellow gown and straw hat, the cut on her cheek cleverly disguised with paint acquired from Sabina the hotel maid. Yet the lady in lilac looked suddenly appalled, as though suspecting herself of unwittingly leading her daughter to a most unrespectable introduction.

Irritated by such a slight to April—and knowing full well the interpretation that could be put on his leaving a hotel at this time of the morning with a beautiful young girl on his arm—Piers said aloofly, "My wife."

The next difficulty of introducing the unknown lady in lilac was then postponed by her astonished cry of, "Your wife! Forgive me, I had no idea your lordship had married! Lady Petteril, how do you do?"

Piers felt the jolt of his own mistake. Heat seeped upward into his face with the too late knowledge that he had not met the woman in Portugal after all, but in England, and she clearly knew exactly who he was.

Fortunately, perhaps—for he could think of nothing to say or do except stalk away—Bertie materialized at his other side.

"Mrs. Larkston, what a delightful surprise," he said. "Have you just arrived in Lisbon? Miss Larkston, your devoted servant."

"How do you do, Major Withan? A great pleasure to see you, but I must beg you at once to write to your aunt Lady Petteril. She is worried sick about you!"

"Is she?" Bertie said without much interest. "Are you staying at Latour's?"

"No, no, we are at the Royal. But my husband the colonel…"

Piers did not hear the rest for his own chaotic thoughts.

He was only aware that a moment later, as he managed to walk disdainfully onward, Bertie said with relief, "Well thank God at least they're not staying in the same place! Rather put your foot in it there, old fellow."

"I've still no idea who she is," Piers said, relaxing. He glanced at April. "Don't worry. If she gossips, people will just assume she got muddled and pity her."

"I wouldn't be too sure," Bertie argued. "Don't you remember her? She's a great crony of Aunt Hortensia's."

"Doesn't matter," April said at once. "She'll just think his lordship's been misbehaving, not with me."

"What if Mrs. Larkston sees you in London trotting about after him?" Bertie said, amused. "Or visits his lordship in company with my aunt? Best lie low for a bit."

"Don't be daft," April scoffed. Only the slip of her accent revealed her sudden discomfort. "No one cares."

Distractedly, Piers patted her hand. Much more socially aware than his family suspected, he already knew he had a problem. And no means of solving it. None that he liked, at any rate. And certainly none that she would.

BREAKFAST WAS ALMOST hectically cheerful, a fact Piers acknowledged from a distance as he thought through his own and April's problems while nodding agreement as Bertie solved his, with the agreement of the starry-eyed Eliana.

"If the doctors pass me fit," Bertie said, "I'll join the army immediately. If possible, I'd like to go out with Everett next week. I need to be doing something."

"You will take care?" Elianna asked anxiously. "And you will write to me?"

"I shall do both," Bertie promised. "On one condition."

"What?" Eliana asked with her first sign of uncertainty.

"Don't marry anyone else in the next few months. Don't run away to your dashed nunnery. And make sure your parents don't hide my letters. Or your own replies."

"How should she do that?" Piers asked, roused from his own issues.

"Send them via Sabina," April said. "She is the maid at Latour's and very romantic by nature."

"You're not just a pretty face, are you?" Bertie said admiringly.

April opened her mouth. Piers waited for her expected truculent reply, *"I ain't pretty."* It never came. She closed her mouth and Bertie moved on.

"I'm not quite myself," he said to Eliana. "Even when I am, I'll have little enough to offer, but we can be friends until we can decide what is best for us."

"And beyond that, too, I hope," Eliana said shyly.

"NEVER THOUGHT BERTIE would show such good sense," Piers remarked an hour later when he and April were finally alone in their room.

She walked to the sofa, oddly restless, and sat down. "Well, it probably helps that she's rich as that cove whose name I can't remember."

"Croesus," Piers said, "and your accent's slipped."

"Who cares?" she retorted. "We're going home soon, aren't we?"

"We'll wait and see Bertie off with Everett. If he's fit to go. But we should, as Bertie suggested, lie low until we leave."

"Don't see why," she muttered. "Are you still thinking of that Mrs. Larkston and her big mouth?"

"More about my big mouth," he said ruefully. "Sorry, April, I'd no idea who she was."

She shrugged. She understood that he never recognized anyone, accepted it without judgement. "I should have warned you I didn't know her. That way at least you'd have known you'd met her in England and not here. We got a bit...blasé."

He couldn't help the smile that quirked his lips. "We did. We may excuse ourselves on the grounds of having much on our minds, namely Bertie."

"What'll happen to the condessa?" April demanded, deliberately changing the subject.

He let her, for the moment. "I don't know yet. I doubt they will make public any of this mess, which reflects well on no one. At the very least, I imagine her trade with the French will be stopped, though to give her due, I wouldn't be surprised if she wasn't curtailing that herself already. In her own way, she is loyal to her country." He regarded April. "*She* knows you as Lady Petteril too. Half the Envoy's staff will by now. And Everett's cronies."

"They don't matter, they're all in Portugal. Besides, the condessa is a foreigner and a traitor and she kept your cousin drugged and imprisoned for weeks. She doesn't count."

"They all count," Piers said. "The thing is, we have a problem, April. Word will spread—is already spreading—that you have been living with me as my wife since we left England."

"I missed that part," April retorted. "You never laid a finger on me."

"Don't pretend to be naïve. That's not what people will assume. It's certainly not what my aunt will think. Nor Mr. and Mrs. Park." The latter were his butler and housekeeper at the London house who had taken April under their wing, civilized her as best they could, and looked out for her against any nasty accusations from other servants.

"They never thought any such thing before. They know you're just eccentric and I'm no one."

"April, this is beyond you being my groom or my assistant. No one else will employ you now. Except, *maybe*, Lady Haggard. No one will marry you, not even your William."

"He's not my William and I don't want to marry him. I don't want to marry anyone, or work for anyone else."

"April, you can't work for me now," he said gently. "Your reputation is gone."

She whitened, though she turned her head away toward the window to hide the fact. "Doesn't matter. No one needs to know who I am."

"Mrs. Larkston could easily recognize you. And the Envoy and his staff. It's a smaller world than you think."

"I'll go if I'm not useful anymore," she muttered. "I'm used to looking after myself."

"April!" He threw himself down beside her, seizing her by the chin to make her look at him. "I'm not going to throw you out in the street. We're friends, aren't we?"

"Always," she whispered, and he ached to take her in his arms.

Instead, he dropped his hand on his knee. "Then we have to decide what to do. As I see it, you have several choices."

"I'm not going to like any of them, am I?" she said with a trace of humour that almost broke his heart.

"No," he admitted. "To own the truth, I don't like them much myself, but we can make them work and still have fun."

She swallowed, then waved one hand elaborately for him to proceed.

"I can find a cottage for you in the country, or something in London if you prefer, with an annuity that will enable you to live."

She stared at him. "Like Annie?"

"Not quite like Annie," he said, for Annie was April's courtesan friend with a small house of her own in Kensington. "But you would be independent."

"Not if I was taking your money for nothing, I wouldn't."

"You would be giving me peace of mind. The faults that led us here are mine. But that is only one choice, and you should consider it carefully with the others."

"What are the others?"

"I'm afraid," he said apologetically, "those involve marrying me."

She laughed aloud. "Don't talk daft! The likes of you do *not* marry the likes of me."

"That is true, as a rule. Such an unequal marriage would be awkward for you and lonely, for society would never do more than tolerate you and snigger behind your back. You need not care for such people, but I doubt you would be very comfortable."

"I wouldn't," she agreed. "And the third?"

"You still marry me, but we disguise you somehow. We pretend you are some foreign noblewoman in distress, met abroad and taken home to England. We might have to take a few people like the Parks into our confidence—and Bertie, of course, who will go along with us from gratitude and schoolboy honour. Others might see odd similarities between you and April, but with a new voice and accent, perhaps a different colour of hair and a very different manner—you are a fine actress as we have already discovered—I believe we could pull it off. The small-minded like my aunt would just assume I had a *type*."

She closed her mouth, staring at him. "That's the one you like best, isn't it?"

"Yes," he admitted. "No one would look down on you. You could make friends and grow into your role. You could be *contented*, or at least become so quite quickly. It will take some setting up and string pulling but it can be done."

She stood up as if she could not bear to be near him and strode to the window. At least she didn't rush out of the room.

"I won't touch you," he said unwisely. "I propose a marriage in name only."

"Because I'm corrupted and disgusting."

He closed his eyes. "No. Because you deserve consideration. We would just continue as we are—like this, where we still have fun, but are married in truth."

Still she did not turn. Her little body was rigid.

"Not in truth. In lies," she said in a cold, hard voice.

"Yes," he agreed. "But only to others. Not between us."

His heart beat with a weird anxiety he had never known before. Already, he was planning ahead, how to build the story of her past life and obtain the necessary documents, how to stop her running away... *Would* she run away from him now? No, she trusted him.

But would she agree?

She did not speak. Her back remained to him. He had thrown too much at her too quickly and he knew from experience she did not like change. He imagined her happiness, her sunny nature slipping away, and hated himself for his ineptitude. How could he have done this to her? From well-meaning stupidity...

At last, he rose to his feet. "Think about it carefully, April," he said gently. "Consider all the choices, and if you have better ideas, tell me those, too."

"I don't need to think about it." Abruptly, she turned from the window. Her eyes were huge in her pale face, the cut on her cheek visible again, because her silent tears had washed off the paint. She dashed her sleeve against her cheek, once more the street urchin who hated showing weakness of any kind. "I can't live with you dishonestly, so I won't be your exotic foreign wife. And I can't take your money for nothing. So, I'll go away and look after myself."

"April—" He started toward her, but she threw up one hand, warding him off.

"You claim it's my choice," she said fiercely. "And that's the sensible one. We both know it. I'll probably stay. I like Portugal. I could be content here. I'd even write to you if you wrote back."

Panic surged inside him. "April, I can't abandon you alone in a foreign country!"

"Why, because it ain't right? Well, neither is *you* marrying *me*. What's more, I can't be where I'm not wanted, and I'm not. Not as your wife."

He felt her pain as if it was his, felt her slipping away, lost, if he could not change this. "You've been my wife for more than a fortnight. It's actually more comfortable than master and servant."

Her mouth opened as if to disparage, then closed again. A frown tugged at her brow as she gazed at him.

"Comfortable," she repeated, her tone unreadable. And yet something was going on in her mind. "Why did you say you didn't like any of these choices?"

"Because I knew you would not."

Her gaze intensified. Her breath caught, yet still she didn't look away. He was reminded of the first time he tried to send her away and she had fought tooth and nail to stay. She had known then he was attempting to save her from himself and she would not allow it. Now, he was trying to save her again, but this time by binding her closer. And it seemed she would not allow that either.

Her tongue crept out, swept over her lips, which moved as if trying out words. Huge, terrifying words.

"So I could go off on my own," she said aloud, careful and precise. "*Or*... I'll marry you as I am. Honestly. I can take the contempt if you can take the ridicule."

He stared at her, because she could always, always surprise him. And yet, the pain he felt now was only an echo of what was to come.

"Which would you prefer?" he asked, as though giving her a choice of hats or something equally trivial. It was the only way not to lose her.

After a brief pause for consideration, she replied in the same vein. "On the whole, I'd prefer to marry you."

It was foolish, insane, and yet his heart burst into song, just as it had all those weeks ago when she'd danced alone around his dusty attic, a beautiful angel in ridiculous, ill-fitting clothes.

"Excellent," he managed with aplomb. He even offered her his arm and was madly proud when her fingers slid lightly over his sleeve with no hesitation.

Her gaze flickered up to his. "You know I'll just be another stick for them to beat you with."

"My family? Nonsense." He squared his shoulders and assumed his haughtiest expression. "I am the viscount."

And perhaps for the first time ever, he felt like it.

Watch out for the sixth Lord Petteril Mystery, coming summer 2024!

About the Author

MARY LANCASTER IS A USA Today bestselling author of award winning historical romance and historical fiction. She lives in Scotland with her husband, one of three grown-up kids, and a small dog with a big personality.

Her first literary love was historical fiction, a genre which she relishes mixing up with romance and adventure in her own writing. Several of her novels feature actual historical characters as diverse as Hungarian revolutionaries, medieval English outlaws, and a family of eternally rebellious royal Scots. To say nothing of Vlad the Impaler.

More recently, she has enjoyed writing light, fun Regency romances, with occasional forays into the Victorian era. With its slight change of emphasis, *Petteril's Thief*, was her first Regency-set historical mystery.

CONNECT WITH MARY ON-line – she loves to hear from readers:

Email Mary: Mary@MaryLancaster.com

Website: http://www.MaryLancaster.com

Newsletter sign-up: https://marylancaster.com/newsletter/

Facebook: https://www.facebook.com/mary.lancaster.1656

Facebook Author Page: https://www.facebook.com/MaryLancasterNovelist/

Twitter: @MaryLancNovels https://twitter.com/MaryLancNovels

Bookbub: https://www.bookbub.com/profile/mary-lancaster

Printed in Great Britain
by Amazon

42835985R00098